HOLLYOAKS
A MERSEY TELEVISION CO

COMIN

CW00853932

Adapted from
Phil Redmond's Hollyoaks
by
Karen Dolby

4

A CHANNEL FOUR BOOK

◼ *sapling*

The publishers would like to thank Phil Redmond for his help and advice in producing this book.

First published in Great Britain in 1996 by Sapling, an imprint of Boxtree Limited, Broadwall House, 21 Broadwall, London SE1 9PL

ISBN 0 7522 0145 X

10 9 8 7 6 5 4 3 2 1

A CIP catalogue entry for this book is available from the British Library

Typeset by SX Composing DTP, Rayleigh, Essex
Printed in Great Britain by
Cox & Wyman Ltd, Reading, Berks

Chapter 1

There was a low, mechanical roaring sound as an engine was revved hard. The bushes at the edge of the wood flattened and slowly parted. A startled wood pigeon flapped squawking into the air. The drowsy peace of the afternoon was about to be broken.

A car came careering through the wooded undergrowth and burst out into open parkland on the edge of Chester. It slid sideways to a grinding halt in a hail of gravel and dead leaves, the engine roaring, exhaust billowing with fumes and smoke pumping from under the bonnet. Even before the car stopped, the driver's door was flung open and a teenage boy scrambled out. He was quickly followed by a girl from the passenger seat. The driver threw open one of the back doors and yelled at whoever was inside to get out. As he did, he glanced anxiously at the thickening smoke now beginning to curl out from the back of the car. A second boy staggered from the car and the driver pushed the boy and girl away, shouting at them to run. He turned back to the car and frantically hauled the last passenger from the back seat, half dragging, half carrying her as he raced to get away.

Not a moment too soon. The petrol tank erupted into a ball of fire, the force of the blast blowing the four teenagers off their feet, flinging them on to the ground. They lay stunned. Slowly the two boys stood up and stared in disbelief at the burning car. One of the girls groaned and stood unsteadily. 'Are you O.K. Julie?' Ollie, the driver asked. She nodded and turned to her friend, Sarah. But Sarah lay unmoving and pale. Julie knelt down and tried to wake her.

'She's not . . . ?' Ollie began. Julie sighed with relief as she felt a pulse and quickly shook her head. 'No.'

It was all too much for the other boy. He took a last look at Sarah lying unconscious and still with Julie and Ollie at her side and made a run for the scrubland nearby. Julie and Ollie looked terrified and lost, neither knew what to do next. Their dilemma was about to be solved for them.

Police sirens wailed, coming closer. Ollie hesitated and then grabbed Julie's hand. They ducked down out of sight in long grass seconds before a police car, closely followed by an ambulance, dashed on to the scene.

'How did they get here so fast?' muttered Ollie. Someone must have seen the car careering out of control off the road and into the woods at the edge of the park and dialled 999. Two paramedics wasted no time rushing over to tend Sarah. Scarcely breathing, Ollie and Julie watched from their hiding place. They looked like frightened children, much younger than their fifteen years. Was Sarah going to be all right?

It felt like forever that she was out for, but within seconds Sarah was stirring into consciousness.

'We can't help by staying here,' hissed Ollie. 'Let's go, before we're caught.' The pair slipped quietly away.

Meanwhile, the car blazed and crackled. 'Shame really,' said one of the policemen. 'Someone has put a lot of time and effort into that bonfire.'

The two policemen considered the burning wreck of an old Mark II Ford Consul. You could still make out the matt grey paint and the air-brushed artwork along each side – the flames arching from the front wheels matching the real flames still leaping from the back. There was a distinctive 'Flying Virgin' image printed on the bonnet. The second policeman looked quizzically at it. He had seen it somewhere else recently, but couldn't remember where.

Chapter 2

At the same time as the last flames were doused on the burned-out car, Kurt Benson walked into his bedroom. He was nineteen, dark-haired, wearing jeans and carrying a T-shirt. With his bare, muscly torso it was easy to see why he was never short of girlfriends. Today he was in a hurry and walked purposefully across to his computer. He had put the system together himself and included a scanjet and colour printer. He smiled as he grabbed the printout of the screen image. 'Yes!' he said triumphantly, punching the air. He hit the eject button, grabbed the floppy disk and erased the screen image of what looked like a party invitation. He hurried out pulling on his T-shirt. Holding the floppy disk between his teeth, he slipped into a leather jacket, pushed on an Airi helmet air-brushed with the same 'Flying Virgin' emblem that had been painted on the burning car and rushed down the steps of his parents' Georgian house. The motorbike which he kick-started and the roar as Kurt pulled the bike upright and accelerated away were in total contrast to the staid BMWs and Volvos parked next to the other houses in the leafy, suburban street in Chester. Curtains moved as neighbours watched in disgust.

As Kurt raced off on his bike, Natasha Andersen dashed out of the sixth form college where she was studying for A levels. She stopped, huffing with annoyance as she watched her bus pulling away from the bus stop. 'If only I had the money for enough lessons to pass my driving test I wouldn't have to waste time waiting around for buses, she thought.' She amused herself while waiting for the next bus by trying to decide what car she would like to drive.

Kurt's motorbike roared around the corner just in time to see what looked like Natasha climb aboard a bus. The doors closed and the bus headed off . . . in the opposite direction. Kurt turned the bike 180 degrees, stopping the bike and pivoting it around his leg towards the kerb. He caught the traffic behind by surprise and the pedestrians even more by surprise as he had to mount the pavement and ride along a little way before cutting back into the traffic, crossing to the other side and setting off in hot pursuit of the bus. Natasha, head buried in a magazine, was listening to her walkman. She did not notice the motorbike or the rider coming up alongside, before Kurt had to fall back behind to avoid the oncoming traffic. But at least Kurt knew Natasha was on the bus.

'That's about all I do know,' he thought. He ran through the facts. He knew her name was Natasha; she was seventeen; went to the college where his best mate Tony worked; she had been two years below him at school, only he hadn't really noticed her then; she was now sitting on a bus, heading where – home? That much he knew, that and the fact that she was drop-dead gorgeous and he would like to know more.

Kurt pulled ahead of the bus and was slowing down near the bus stop where he thought Natasha got out when he noticed a passing police car. Unfortunately, the policemen inside seemed to recognize Kurt, or rather, his conspicuous helmet: the fact that his bike had neither tax disc nor number plate and the owner had a notoriously individual approach to riding and road use may also have contributed. Kurt gunned the bike and wheelied away with the police car struggling to do a three-point turn and follow. Kurt, who was not unused to such chases, headed towards the park with the police car in hot pursuit, sirens sounding and blue lights flashing. The motorbike zipped through a small pedestrian gate to the park and vanished over a landscaped bank. The car could not follow and headed off in a bid to intercept the bike at the other gate.

As soon as he was sure the police had gone, Kurt doubled back towards the bus stop where the bus was just pulling out. He could see Natasha walking away in the distance and followed, but just as he was about to catch up with her, she turned on to a footpath towards the river. Kurt stopped the bike and hurried along the path after her. He was in time to see her disappear inside the Dog in the Pond pub. Kurt sighed and swore to himself. After blowing it again he felt a bit of a prat. It would be completely uncool to do anything other than go.

Chapter 3

Kurt headed back to college to find his mate, Tony Hutchinson. Unlike Kurt who had taken a year out before going on to university, Tony was working in the sixth form college canteen as a trainee chef. Tony did not have Kurt's cool confidence and did not want to study any more. He had started a catering course at the college and when he finished was offered a temporary job which drifted into a permanent one because the manager liked him.

Kurt and Tony had been mates since infant school when a six year old Tony saved Kurt from the bullying attention of Ozzie Mac, the primary school thug. They were now both mad on cars and motorbikes and Kurt was trying, very unsuccessfully, to teach Tony to play the guitar. Unlike Kurt, Tony was a bit shy with girls, mainly because he had, as Kurt saw it, the greatest failing for any red-blooded adolescent male – he actually liked and respected women. To top it all, with an older and a younger sister, Kurt also reckoned that Tony had been 'mentally neutered'.

Kurt parked his bike next to Tony's Honda CB125, which was carefully chained next to a down-pipe and fitted with L-plates. He strolled into the canteen kitchen where Tony, dressed in his chef's uniform, made Kurt a cup of tea. They settled on the stainless steel work tops for one of Tony's breaks.

'I don't know why you don't just get rid of that helmet,' Tony said. 'You might as well have a neon sign on your head flashing, "I'm Kurt. Nick me".'

'This is my trophy. It's worth 200 quid,' Kurt protested.

'Come on,' laughed Tony. 'You won it from that bloke who bet you wouldn't ride your bike over the footbridge across the river. It cost you nothing.'

Kurt grinned. 'Anyway, why do the cops keep picking on me?'

'It might have something to do with you breaking the law . . . the police are funny about things like that,' said Tony.

'Ha! Ha! Very funny,' Kurt replied. He fished out the tea bag from his mug and dropped it, still hot, on to Tony's palm.

'So – was it worthwhile then? Did you get to talk to the wonderful Natasha?' asked Tony.

Kurt hesitated, looking just a little embarrassed, 'Almost . . .' then he added defensively. 'I don't want to rush things. Women like to be handled sensitively.'   ·

Tony looked sceptical, 'What you were doing

with Maddie in the back of the Consul last weekend? It didn't sound very sensitive.'

'That's different,' said Kurt. 'Maddie's not a woman . . . she's a sex object. What would the world be without red-blooded males?

'Tidier, prettier, smell nicer . . .' Tony began.

Kurt gave him a withering look, 'Prat!' That was the problem with growing up in a house full of women.

Tony grinned, but looked needled. 'At least I can talk to women,' he said.

'Who wants to talk?' Kurt replied, as the canteen cook walked in. Visitors were not allowed inside the kitchen. Tony and Kurt made for the door.

Tony was still curious as to why Kurt had failed yet again to talk to the delicious Natasha. It was very unlike Kurt to have fancied a girl for as long as this without getting anywhere. Six weeks – he must be losing his touch.

But Kurt did not want to talk about it any more. He flipped the floppy disk to Tony. 'Ask that blurt in the office to run it through the colour copier. Get six, we might as well have some spares.'

Tony looked unsure. Louise had been planning this party for six months and had made it clear she did not want them there.

'You know they'll tumble that we forged the tickets,' Tony said.

'But we'll be in by then. And Louise is not the type to want a fuss, is she? Then I can make a move on Natasha.' As he spoke, Kurt's attention was caught by two figures coming around the corner. It was Ollie, Kurt's younger brother and his girlfriend, Julie.

Ollie saw Kurt, did a U-turn and started to make off in the opposite direction. Before he got far, Kurt shouted at him to come back. There seemed to be something wrong.

'Ollie!' Kurt called. 'What happened to you?'

Ollie seemed at a loss for words. Julie answered for him. 'We've been in an accident . . .'

'What have you done *this* time, Ollie?' asked Kurt, immediately the big brother. 'How bad is it?'

Julie carried on talking. 'Sarah, my schoolfriend, is in hospital.'

'Let's have it fast. The full story,' Kurt said sternly.

After a short silence, Ollie found his voice and what happened tumbled out. 'It was an accident. I thought we were gonna be there and back before you ever found out and you'd never notice the car was gone . . . and then it caught fire, right . . . I had to ditch it . . .' Kurt's face was a picture of disbelief. Ollie started to back away.

'The car? . . . *the* car. Not just any old car?' Kurt roared. 'You trashed *my* car!?!'

Ollie grimaced and tried to make his head shrink into his body as he attempted to nod.

Kurt began quietly. 'You took . . . my car?

You've smashed up my car . . . and put someone in hospital with it?'

Ollie couldn't find the breath to speak. He nodded, waiting for the eruption. With a rumbling growl Kurt lunged at Ollie.

Chapter 4

Natasha was on her way to see her friend, Dawn
Cunningham, who had been having almost as
bad a day as Kurt. Because of tensions at home,
Dawn often stayed over at Natasha's. Dawn had
left school after A levels and now worked in
Rose Parker's interior design shop in one of
Chester's Dickensian alleys.

At the same time that Kurt's prized car had
been exploding into a ball of fire, Dawn had
been leaving work. It was her afternoon for finishing early and as she sprang down the steps of
the shop she smiled to herself. Work had been
fun and now she was looking forward to a few
hours of free time . . . and, more importantly,
Louise's party that night. As she was walking
along, a car with a sign saying Cunningham
Driving School pulled up next to her. The
middle-aged man inside gently sounded the
horn. She turned and waved at the driver. It
was her father, Gordon. Dawn did not see her
father nearly as much as she would have liked.
Dawn's mother, Angela, hated Gordon with a
passion and made it very difficult for any of her

children to see him.

Dawn climbed into the car and they chatted about all the usual everyday things they missed knowing about each other now they no longer lived in the same house. Dawn told him about work and friends, and what her brother and sister were up to at school. She carefully avoided anything about her mother or more particularly about her mother's creepy boyfriend, Terry. An hour passed quickly and since Gordon had to pick up his next pupil, he drove Dawn home. As Dawn was leaning into the car to say goodbye, her mother appeared at the door. She spotted the car, her eyes lit up and she froze, furious. In a blind rage, she grabbed a milk bottle from the step and raced down the garden path towards the car. Dawn saw her father looking past her in alarm. He quickly said goodbye and sped away at top speed. In the nick of time, Dawn realized what was happening and desperately tried to stop her mother who nevertheless managed to throw the bottle. It smashed on the pavement a few feet away. Dawn and Angela glared at one another, both equally strong-willed. Finally Dawn strode into the house in disgust. Angela stood alone watching the car disappear from view.

When Natasha arrived at the house, Dawn was clearing up the glass from the street. Natasha took one look at her friend's pale, strained face and the glass and recognized an old problem.

'What happened this time?' she asked, bending down to help.

'The usual,' Dawn sighed. 'The mother from hell drawing on all those years as a trained trauma counsellor giving a practical demonstration on how "not to internalize one's problems", "how not to bottle things up", but instead "how to release pent-up frustration" and act like a raving lunatic . . . She saw me talking to Dad.'

Natasha followed Dawn into the house. 'I know it was your Dad who had the affair but it's years since they divorced. Do you think she'll ever forgive him?'

'She'd prefer to be a martyr than consider that she was even the tiniest bit to blame. The problem has always been that she's so busy giving emotional support to the people she counsels that she never sees anything wrong at home with any of us. She never has. She's always been elsewhere. She never noticed Dad was unhappy. That's why he had the affair in the first place. And unlike her, he's been on his own ever since the break up, not with some creep . . .' Dawn finished bitterly as the creep appeared in the doorway. This was Terry. At twenty-nine he was fifteen years younger than Dawn's mother. Wearing jeans, a tight vest and a gold earring and with his leering appraisal of Natasha, he looked every bit a creep. He blew in Natasha's ear and waved the phone at her. Natasha's face hardened as she took the phone

15

and turned her back on him.

The expression on Natasha's face quickly changed to one of horror as she listened.

'What's happened?' Dawn asked anxiously when Natasha switched off the phone.

'Sarah's in hospital,' Natasha looked very shocked.

'Your sister Sarah?'

Natasha nodded. 'She's been in a car crash or something. I'm going to the hospital.'

'I'm coming with you,' said Dawn.

Chapter 5

A little after Natasha and Dawn arrived at the hospital, two other figures made their way to the Accident and Emergency Department. They were Kurt and Ollie, the latter looking very uncomfortable. Kurt was trying to get an honest explanation from Ollie about what had happened.

'I've told you, it was an accident. I didn't know you only had a temporary fuel line on the thing,' Ollie said, defensively.

'You had no need to know. You were not supposed to be driving my car,' Kurt replied.

Just then Ollie spotted Sarah coming out of a side cubicle, with a doctor, a policeman and a man who was obviously her father. Although she looked quite shaken and a bit wobbly, she did not appear to be seriously hurt. It seemed that her father was taking her home. Kurt was still carrying his very noticeable 'Flying Virgin' helmet and side-stepped into a doorway with Ollie to avoid being seen by the policeman.

'She looks O.K.,' whispered Ollie, cheering up.

'Luckily for you,' snapped Kurt. 'Now –

would you mind telling me exactly what happened and exactly what state my car is in?'

'It was all Dogger's fault,' Ollie began. Kurt looked sceptical. 'Well you see . . . he said I wouldn't dare do it,' Kurt still looked sceptical. 'He bet me fifty quid, his birthday money, so I took the keys . . .' Ollie trailed off as he saw two girls walking towards them along the corridor.

Kurt turned, 'Er hi . . . Natasha,' he said, trying to appear cool.

'You wouldn't have anything to do with my sister being here, would you?' she asked Ollie suspiciously. Ollie looked as if he wished the ground would swallow him.

'Ah . . . So you have a sister? Is she . . . er . . . is she . . .' Kurt fished for the right words.

'Forget it, Benson,' Natasha said, very coolly.

Kurt watched miserably as the two girls left. He turned on Ollie in silence. Ollie assumed the worst, basically that Kurt was thinking of the slowest and most painful form of death for him. Unable to stand the suspense, he blurted out, backing away, 'What!? What are you going to do to me?'

Kurt smiled, winding Ollie up. 'Why should I do anything? I'll only get thrown into jail . . . for assault . . . or worse . . . Not me,' he pointed towards Natasha's disappearing figure. 'If she decides to tell the cops, which she obviously hasn't done yet, they'll deal with you.' With that Kurt headed for the door, leaving Ollie to trudge home alone.

Chapter 6

Later that evening Tony took the forged invitations to Kurt's house. As usual they sat in Kurt's bedroom, which was in its customary mess. Laundry littered the floor and the walls were masked by images from every stage of Kurt's life – there were road signs, posters for the Ducati Monster, Triumph Speed Triple, Thunderbird and the Hoss Boss; one wall was covered with 'liberated' Adshell posters and there was even an old plaster cast. The computer system was set up on an improvised work station and was also hooked up to a keyboard and multi-track.

Kurt was flopped on the bed studying the invitations, while Tony struggled to pick out a bar G chord on the acoustic guitar. Next to him on its stand stood Kurt's pride and joy – his Fender Sunburst Stratocaster.

'The paper's a bit heavier than the real ones but once we crease them up – pretty passable,' Kurt grinned and pointed to the computer. 'Ain't technology wonderful?'

'Why was Ollie at college today?' Tony asked.

'Coming to see you. He didn't know I'd be there and thought . . .' Kurt paused.

'I'd break it to you gently?' Tony finished. 'What's happening about the car?'

'I reported it "missing" to the police. Otherwise I wouldn't be able to get any money on the insurance.'

They were interrupted by the sash window sliding open. A woolly hatted head appeared.

'Wotcha chaps,' It was Jambo Bolton. He climbed inside as if this was the way everyone should enter a room. Kurt and Tony were used to this strange habit and showed no surprise. Kurt held out the invitations for Jambo to look at. He was impressed but not by Tony's strumming. Tony had switched to a straight 'G' at Kurt's suggestion.

'That's rubbish,' Jambo said to Tony. 'I mean, have you ever tried bar chords . . . all you have to do is slide your hand up and down . . . like that . . .' Jambo demonstrated, making it look easy. Then he flicked the invites back to Kurt and went to pick up the Stratocaster. Tony froze, waiting for the reaction. He shook his head warningly at Jambo. No one was allowed to touch Kurt's Strat. Jambo registered the mistake and stopped.

'Hey! Would I?' he joked. 'Look – a speck of dust.' He flicked the scratch plate gently. 'I take it these tickets mean we're in tonight? Still going to make a move on Nat . . . Nat . . . Natasha?'

Jambo was distracted by the appearance of Kurt's younger sister. Kurt looked irritated, Tony a bit embarrassed and Jambo looked like it was Christmas.

'How many times have I told you that the point of having a door is to stop you falling over when you go to knock to ask if it's O.K. to come in,' said Kurt.

'"Knock" it off Kurt – I've seen it all before,' Lucy snapped.

'Not mine you haven't . . . but if you really want to . . .' Jambo grinned.

'Ha! Ha!' Lucy said in a bored voice, turning to Kurt. 'I didn't realize the missing link had swung in again. You should stop feeding him bananas . . . There's someone to see you downstairs. A policeman as a matter of fact.'

The atmosphere in the room suddenly changed completely. Jambo made for the window, Tony looked worried and Kurt pensive.

'He wants a word with you, Kurt,' Lucy explained, puzzled.

Kurt grabbed Jambo with one hand and Tony sighed with relief.

'Will you all relax. I just reported my car was missing – O.K.?' Kurt said.

'I'd better bring him up then,' Lucy looked alarmed as she rushed to the door.

'Not in here you don't,' said Kurt, glancing around the room at the traffic signs and odd bits of contraband on the walls. He quickly threw something on to the bed to cover his crash helmet. 'I'll come down.'

Lucy left and Jambo followed, leaning over the banisters to watch her go. Kurt pulled him back inside his room. 'Stay here!' he said, firmly. 'The last thing I need is Freddy Krueger's younger brother dropping out of a window on top of a police car . . . And . . .' he continued, poking his finger at Jambo. 'That . . . was my sister. O.K.?'

'Even if I promise never to touch your Strat again. Ever?' Jambo enquired, grinning.

Kurt turned to Tony. 'You're a witness, Tony. I was at the canteen with you! It's yes sir, no sir . . .'

Jambo sat down on the bed to wait. He began to pick out a tune on the acoustic guitar. It was through their shared interest in music that Jambo had first met Kurt and Tony. Kurt had been the leader of a local headline band – until he dated the drummer's girlfriend, who was also the bass player's sister and keyboard's cousin. Jambo had been at the gig during which the drummer found out about Kurt and his girlfriend and enjoyed the ensuing punch-up better than the set. He'd waded in to help Kurt initially because he could not see the merit of three musicians 'licking seven scales out of one guitarist', but he also confessed later that he had always wanted to hit Buddy Butter – Jambo's nickname for the drummer. Jambo had an individual, anarchic attitude to life and was his own man. This did not stop him, though, from working hard at his job at the garden centre, where he was popular with the customers for his sense of humour and because he knew a lot about plants.

Chapter 7

At eight o'clock that evening, Dawn arrived at the Dog in the Pond to call for Natasha. Greg, Natasha's father, was in the bar. He smiled when he saw Dawn. 'You're obviously going to Louise's party, too,' he said.

'Not allowed to miss it. She's only been planning it for six months! How's Sarah?'

'She's fine – now,' Greg hesitated. 'You don't know who she was with do you? She won't tell me. Code of silence. Still, she is all right – and she's only got herself to blame for this mess.'

'She is your daughter, too,' Natasha quipped, overhearing Greg's comment as she walked into the bar. She kissed her father, 'See ya' later . . .'

'Wait a minute,' Greg called as the two girls were about to leave. 'How are you getting home?'

'We'll get a lift. Maddie will be there. Don't worry,' she said seeing her father's expression. 'If there's a problem we'll phone.'

The party was being held in a hall with local pirate radio Jungle DJ Bazz FM on disco duty. At eleven o'clock the evening was in full swing and very crowded. Louise, looking distracted, had just found Dawn and Natasha.

'You haven't seen Joe have you?' she asked, before wandering off to continue her search.

'Definitely love, poor girl . . .' shouted Natasha above the music. She stopped as she saw Dawn's expression change. Maddie was cutting a swathe through the crowd with what looked like a trainee building society manager in tow.

'I don't know what she sees in him,' said Natasha.

'It's not his mind she's after,' Dawn answered.

Maddie was the daughter of Rose Parker who owned the interior design shop where Dawn worked. If Natasha was seen as a fair swap for Cindy Crawford, then Maddie was a good substitute for the Wonderbra Woman. Maddie had a definite look of 'come up and see me some time' about her, and she was very capable of looking after herself. She could play the male macho game against the best of them, sometimes making Natasha and Dawn die of embarrassment. Maddie had her own code of conduct and knew exactly what she was doing – including how far she wanted to go, when and with whom. This had one drawback in so far as it had given her an unfortunate reputation as something of a sex beast – although most of that was wishful thinking on the guys' part. Maddie was very clear about what equality and equal opportunities were supposed to be – and what they really were.

'Hi guys. You've met Tom?' Maddie asked.

'Gosh,' said Tom. 'I have to say that you two look marvellous tonight, as always. Though not as delicious as my Maddie.' Tom wound his way through the crowd to find drinks for himself and Maddie.

'What do you see in him?' asked Natasha when he had gone.

'It's not his mind . . .' laughed Maddie, 'I'm after.' Then she remarked 'I see Lou's broken up with her precious Joe.' Seeing Dawn's and Natasha's puzzled expressions she added. 'He's outside by the bins giving the kiss of life to someone.' Natasha and Dawn looked at each other in panic and dashed off.

At the same time, Kurt, Tony and Jambo were standing by the main doors trying to get into the party. Matt, Louise's older brother, was on the door checking invitations with some friends from his university rugby team. Matt was studying Kurt's invites dubiously.

'Perhaps they ran out of paper and had a few more printed up . . . I don't know. Look, it's cool,' Kurt said. Matt took another long look at him. Kurt looked 'cool' in collarless shirt and jacket. Jambo looked oblivious and Tony looked nervous.

The three were about to go into the main hall when the doors swung open and Natasha and Dawn came rushing out. Kurt's heart and face sank as Maddie appeared in the doorway behind them. Jambo and Tony gawped.

'Hi, Kurt,' Maddie smiled before turning to Jambo and Tony. 'Are you wearing ties or are those your tongues?' she paused. 'I thought you were going to call me, Kurt?'

'Er . . . you were out,' Kurt stammered.

Maddie was enjoying the wind-up and watching Kurt's discomfort, 'My machine wasn't. And I waited . . . and waited . . . all by myself.'

Now Kurt knew she was teasing. 'Sorry,' he said. 'I have to go.' Kurt made for the door with Tony following. Jambo hesitated. Should he follow his mates . . . or party? With the memory of Maddie upmost in his mind he headed for the party.

By the time Natasha and Dawn arrived on the scene, Joe had got rather further than the kiss of life. 'Oh no . . . It gets worse . . .' exclaimed Natasha, as a side door opened and Louise appeared.

At first she was too shocked to react, then in disbelief she shouted 'Joe!' Joe froze. His friend took in the situation and hurried away. Louise began to cry.

'You don't own me,' Joe said. Louise's anguish turned to anger. She rushed at Joe intending to hit him. Joe stepped aside and shoved her against the wall. She hit her face, stumbled and fell. Natasha and Dawn rushed forward to help their friend.

'What the hell do you think you're doing?' Dawn yelled.

Joe felt outnumbered and under threat. He

grabbed Dawn and pushed her aside. He was just about to do the same to Natasha when Kurt arrived. He saw what was going on and raced across, hitting Joe squarely in the chest with the flat of his hands. Joe staggered backwards and Kurt turned to help Louise up. Joe seized his opportunity and went to hit Kurt.

'Enough!' Kurt bellowed, facing him. And it was. Joe looked at Kurt and at Louise, who was now sobbing. He saw the expressions of contempt on Natasha's and Dawn's faces and decided it would be better if he left.

'Are you O.K.?' Kurt asked Louise.

'Yes,' she said, still sobbing. 'But I'm going home.'

'I'll go with you,' Dawn said immediately. Natasha was about to follow.

'Wait a minute,' Kurt said. 'She'll be O.K. with . . .' He trailed off, not remembering Dawn's name.

'Dawn,' Natasha said. 'I should go . . .' Kurt surreptitiously waved at Tony to disappear.

'Well, of course, if you want to . . .' he said. 'I thought I could walk with you . . . talk about today . . . at the hospital.' Natasha thought for a moment and then agreed. Kurt could hardly believe his luck.

The walk home was all too short. The conversation about the day's events was only just finishing as the Dog in the Pond came into view.

'Ollie felt he couldn't back down. Like an idiot he took on the bet,' Kurt finished.

'So your brother is totally blameless. It was Sarah's boyfriend, Dogger, who caused the whole thing?' Natasha was sceptical.

'At least Ollie didn't run off without seeing if she was all right,' Kurt said in his defense. Natasha nodded. 'It looks like your sister is as good a judge of men as your friend Louise. You nearly lost a sister – I lost my car.'

'It is *only* a car,' Natasha said, teasing.

Kurt protested. 'Only a car. I spent three years putting that car together.'

'A car can be replaced. The insurance money will buy you a new one,' Natasha pointed out. 'It wouldn't have bought me a new sister.'

Kurt accepted this and apologized for what happened.

'It's not you who should apologize,' said Natasha. 'But thank you. And thank you for tonight.'

There was an awkward silence as they glanced at one another feeling suddenly uncertain. They were now at the pub door. Kurt was desperate to continue the moment – not to let her disappear.

'So this is home,' he said, trying to think of things to say and spoiling the understanding that had built up between them. 'Living in a pub – cool.'

'We live upstairs – above the pub,' said Natasha, in charge of the situation now.

'Well . . . seeing as I'm getting tongue-tied and saying stupid things, I'll go.'

Natasha opened the door and grinned. 'Well you can stay, if you like.'

Kurt thought he was dreaming. Then Natasha continued, 'I'm sure no one will mind you standing here by yourself, so long as you don't make a noise.'

Kurt took the joke and went to say goodbye. There was another awkward moment as they stood looking at one another, Natasha in the lit doorway, Kurt in the dark outside. Kurt tried not to look at her extremely kissable lips and wondered if he should or should not kiss her goodnight. Natasha wondered if he would or would not kiss her. While secretly hoping that he at least wanted to, Natasha was well aware of Kurt's reputation with women and had no desire to become just another conquest.

Her mind made up, she said quickly, 'Don't even think about it, Benson.'

'What?' asked Kurt, innocently.

'About whether to try and kiss me or not,' and with that Natasha was gone, leaving Kurt alone outside, staring at the door.

He sighed, 'I guess this isn't one of my better days.' He was about to go when he thought better of it. He was not the type to give up easily and Natasha was definitely worth fighting for. He was smiling as he stepped purposefully back to the door and rang the bell. He was still smiling when the door opened and Kurt saw, not Natasha, but her father and his pet guard dog, Buddy.

Chapter 8

It was rather early in the day, but as far as Kurt was concerned he was gigging live on stage to an adoring audience. He was belting out a post-Nirvana self-composed 'Benson Teen Anthem' inspired by Oasis' 'Rock 'N' Roll Star'. He came to the big chord climactic end of set, jump finishing on the finale. As he landed he looked up and noticed the time. It was nine-thirty in the morning. He should have been somewhere else. He unhooked his Fender and dropped it back on its stand which created an ear-splitting feedback howl. Kurt hit the power switch and left, fast.

He ran outside, colliding with Ollie and his mates. He pulled on his helmet and roared away on his motorbike. Five minutes later, Kurt was waiting impatiently for traffic lights to change. As they finally switched to red and amber, he spotted the police car opposite. At the same moment, they noticed him looking in their direction and recognized his infamous helmet. Kurt pulled away and the siren sounded. The chase was on once more. The situation seemed desperate. There were queues of traffic and progress was slow. Kurt looked around for an escape . . . and smiled. He slid the bike around and, finding a gap in the traffic, gunned across the road to a set of steps. All the police could do was watch in frustration as Kurt pushed the bike up the steps and bumped his way down the other side of a pedestrian bridge over a railway line. Riding away, Kurt raised his fist in triumph 'Ye-es!' However, he was now even later.

Natasha was pacing anxiously up and down outside college, looking at her watch. Thoroughly fed up with the wait, she gave a final glance at her wrist, spun around and hurried into college for her first lesson. An hour later, her lesson finished, she wandered up and down the corridor searching for someone in the crowd. Where was Louise?

Kurt meanwhile had arrived at the garden centre and found Jambo. Too late to sort out Kurt's car which was what they had arranged to do first thing that morning.

'I had a bit of bother on the way,' Kurt explained.

'I've got to deliver this by ten so we'll have to sort out the car after that,' Jambo tied up the back of a loaded flat-back truck. 'I'll meet you behind the Ferret pub in an hour.' Kurt nodded and decided to leave his motorbike in the staff car park. It was too dangerous out on the streets.

* * *

Tony had a mission of his own that morning, one that was taking all his willpower to go through with. He turned his Honda into a street of Georgian, terraced houses. He slowed as he checked the numbers and finally stopped outside one with a green door, Number 20. Should he call? While he was still deciding, Julie came out of the house. It was now or never. Julie began to walk down the street. Then Ollie and three of his friends appeared around the corner. Tony realized he had missed his chance and rode off.

Kurt and Jambo piled into the truck and drove off to see an old mate of Jambo's who worked in a garage not far away. Kurt watched Jambo talk to a guy in the maintenance bay. After a few minutes Jambo nodded and slapped the guy on the shoulder. He sauntered back to Kurt.

'All sorted,' he grinned. They now had a recovery truck organized to pick up Kurt's car. Twenty minutes later they stood surveying the charred wreckage.

'Not a pretty sight, mate,' Jambo commiserated. Kurt nodded. The paintwork had been burnt off and although most of the windows were still in place as the doors had been open when the car exploded, they were blackened by smoke. The interior was badly charred. Half the back seat was burnt and there was some crumpling of the body panels around the petrol tank which had ruptured in the heat. The two rear tyres had gone but the front ones seemed all right and Jambo's mate, Ben, positioned the recovery truck ready to lift the back of the car. He planned to tow it on the front wheels. Kurt tried not to think of the work he had put into the car – the time and effort.

'What does Ben want for letting us use the truck, then?' Kurt asked. 'Two bags of peat and a Metasequoia – for his dad's birthday,' came the reply. 'It's O.K. I can get you trade discount.'

Kurt was touched. 'You know all those times when I've called you a dickhead in the past . . . I meant it – affectionately.'

'Is that the closest you'll get to a "thank you Jambo"?' Jambo grinned.

'Hey! Don't push me,' Kurt also grinned.

'Not even about how you really got on with Nat . . . Nat . . . Natasha,' Jambo asked.

Especially not about that. All Kurt would say was that 'We understand each other.' Jambo did not look too impressed.

Kurt continued, 'Jam, my boy. When you've had as much experience with women as I have, you'll know when to push . . .'

'And when to push off!' Jambo laughed. Jambo knew he had said enough and changed the subject to what they were doing that night.

'Thought we might check out Bazz FM,' Kurt said, with practised nonchalance.

Jambo was immediately suspicious. 'But you think he's sad.'

'He's cool,' said Kurt. 'It's his taste in music that's sad.'

Suddenly Jambo knew what Kurt was up to. Bazz FM must be playing at the Dog in the Pond, Natasha's dad's pub. What a coincidence! Kurt grinned. Jambo might just be right.

They deposited Kurt's car on the drive outside his house.

'It looks like I felt after Louise's party,' said Jambo checking over the mess as he finished a mug of coffee. 'I had something that didn't suit my metabolism. Woke up the next day in next door's garden shed. My boots were covered in green powder. I don't know where I'd been. Anyway, that's my lunch break over.'

Kurt went to take the mugs back inside. He had to go to the garden centre with Jambo to collect his bike. Jambo jumped into the truck and when Kurt reappeared ready to go he started the engine, grinning and waving as he drove away leaving Kurt stranded. A little annoyed, Kurt shook his head wondering about Jambo's twisted sense of humour.

At lunch time Natasha went to the canteen still looking out for Louise. There was no sign of her. Tony was collecting plates and Natasha hurried across.

'You haven't seen Louise Taylor have you?' she asked.

'Was she the one whose party we . . .' Tony trailed off.

'Gatecrashed is the word you're looking for, but yes,' Natasha finished.

Tony had not seen her either. Natasha looked around in the vain hope that Louise might appear. She then took her mobile and tried to phone her home but there was no reply. It was not at all like Louise to miss college and if she was at home, why was she not answering the phone? Now feeling extremely concerned, Natasha dashed off to try to find out.

Louise lived in a 1930s detached mock-Tudor house where everything always looked neat and orderly, from the tidy lawn and straight flower borders to the carefully raked gravel drive and gleaming door knocker. Natasha held her finger on the door bell which she could hear ringing inside the house. Next she tried hammering on the knocker and calling through the letter box. There was no reply. She stepped back and looked up at the house. Clean windows shone back blankly. She was sure the house was empty. There was no point in hanging around but she hesitated. Where should she try next? She went to search out Dawn.

When Natasha arrived at the interior design shop, Dawn was sitting on one of two elegant sofas talking to a customer about wallpaper. Several sample books were open on a coffee table. Dawn gestured to Natasha to wait. Soft chamber music was playing in the background. Natasha ran her hand over one of the expensive-looking fabrics draped artistically on one wall. Nothing in the shop looked out of place. Everything was beautifully designed and displayed. Dawn excused herself.

'What are you doing here?' she asked Natasha.

'You haven't seen Louise, have you?' Natasha asked in a hushed voice. Dawn hadn't. Natasha continued. 'You know what she's been like since catching Joe with that girl?'

'The broken-hearted heroine,' Dawn sighed. 'Joe's a swine. I don't know how many times I've told her.'

'I know,' said Natasha. 'We all have. But now – she's missing.' Dawn looked surprised. 'She's not in college, which is completely unlike her, she's not at home and she's not here.'

'She's never here,' said Dawn.

'That's not the point. We arranged to meet outside the gate this morning and she didn't show up. And,' Natasha paused. 'She was really down last night. That's why I said I'd meet her on the way in to college.'

'How down is down?' asked Dawn. Natasha pointed to floor level. The two girls looked very seriously at each other before Dawn said the unthinkable. 'As in "suicidal" down?'

'No!' said Natasha quickly. Then reluctantly. 'Well . . . maybe.'

'How . . . maybe?'

'Possibly . . .'

'Really?'

Natasha just nodded.

Dawn turned to the customer, pulling on her coat as she spoke. 'I'm afraid you'll have to excuse me. I have to go out. One of my friends is about to kill herself!'

Natasha showed a bewildered customer to the door while Dawn took the quickest route out, stepping on the coffee table, on to the back of the sofa, leaping off the sofa and landing at the door. The two girls walked briskly away back to Louise's house.

Dawn rang the bell and then hammered at the door. Natasha waited impatiently on the drive and also kept an eye out for neighbours wondering what all the noise was about. Finally fed up with waiting and impatient to carry on the search, Natasha said, 'See? She's not here.'

Dawn thought for a moment and then asked, 'Where would you kill yourself?'

Natasha looked shocked but replied, 'In the bath. It's clean and not messy. Although I'd like to be found before I went all wrinkly and prune-like.'

'I'll remember that,' said Dawn. 'But Louise wouldn't do that. It's too practical. She'd want somewhere more romantic.' She thought for a moment. 'Poison?'

Natasha stared at the house, eyes wide. 'Asleep on her bed?!' she whispered.

Dawn looked at the house then shook her head dismissing the idea. 'No. Not dramatic enough. I mean, only her parents would find her.'

They were not getting very far. Dawn was quite right. Louise liked drama and poetic tragedy. Where would a romantic heroine end it all?

'What book is she reading at the moment?' asked Natasha. In answer to Dawn's querying look she added, 'I thought it might be a link.'

'It's more likely to be linked to where she first met Joe,' said Dawn.

The answer came to both girls at the same moment.

'The river!' they exclaimed in unison and raced off.

They ran to the bridge not knowing what to expect. They were certainly not prepared for the sight that met their eyes. Their guess was right. Louise had gone to the bridge. Horrified, Dawn and Natasha saw her climb on to the top of the rail where she leaned forward. She was going to jump!

Natasha and Dawn flew across the bridge. Just in time they grabbed Louise. She almost slipped but they pulled her back to safety.

'What are you doing?!!' Louise wailed. 'You almost killed me.'

'We saved you!' Dawn exclaimed.

'What?' Louise looked at her friends as if they were mad. 'You nearly knocked me off the edge.' With that she held tightly to the hand rail.

Dawn and Natasha looked puzzled and then rather sheepish. 'We thought . . . we thought you were going to kill yourself,' they explained.

Louise started at them both, bewildered. She realized as they let her go and from their weak, apologetic smiles that they actually had thought she was going to do it. Louise gazed down at the river, swaying faintly at the very idea of it. Dawn and Natasha grabbed her again just in case.

'Get off,' said Louise, pushing them away. 'Are you crazy? How could you think I'd do that?'

'Well you were really down,' Natasha tried to explain. 'And when you didn't turn up for college . . .'

'I'd been to the doctor's,' Louise sounded offended and angry.

Dawn, feeling foolish and embarrassed, looked at Natasha if she was an idiot. Natasha tried to defend herself, 'I thought, you know, because of Joe . . .'

'Shut up!' said Dawn.

Natasha, cringing at her mistake said rather crossly, 'Well what are you doing up there then?' Dawn had to admit she had a point and both girls looked at Louise for an explanation.

Louise pointed to a photograph wedged on the bridge railings above her. She reached up to grab it and handed the photo to Dawn. It was from the Haunted House at Alton Towers and showed Joe with his arm around Louise in the front seat with Natasha and Dawn sitting behind.

'I was discarding my memories of him,' Louise stated theatrically. Dawn had been right about the romantic heroine bit.

Natasha and Dawn stared down over the rail. They could still see pieces of torn up photographs floating away on the murky water. Louise was about to send this memory to join all the others when Natasha grabbed it.

'Can't I keep it?' she asked. 'It was a brilliant day. Maybe I could just tear him out of the picture?'

Louise was determined. She ripped the paper across and then held her hand over the rail. She watched the pieces fall like petals onto the water below. She sighed.

'Is that why you went to the doctor? asked Dawn. 'To organize the lobotomy to remove any memories of Joe?'

Louise was not impressed. She gave her a withering look and walked away.

'Idiot,' said Dawn to Natasha before following Louise.

Kurt had an uneventful ride back from the garden centre after collecting his bike. It was a welcome break from police chases and dodging recognition. At home a letter was waiting for him. He tore open the envelope. It was from the car insurance company. As Kurt read, his expression changed to one of fury.

'Ollie!!' he roared. Grabbing his helmet he dashed out.

Tony was again trying to pluck up the courage to speak to Julie. He had liked her for ages but she had been going out with Ollie. After what had happened with the car crash she had not seemed too keen on Ollie and now Tony thought he stood a chance. At least he hoped so.

Tony rode to Julie's street, he slowed the Honda and looked at Julie's front door – then he carried on past. He could hear his heart pounding above the noise of the engine. This was ridiculous. All he had to do was knock on the door and speak to her. Tony was glad no one knew he was there or could see him behaving like an idiot. His mind made up, he turned the bike around and stopped near to the house. Again he hesitated. Perhaps she still liked Ollie? Perhaps she did not like him? Tony's deliberations were cut short by the familiar whine of Kurt's Yamaha tearing up the road. Kurt screeched to a halt, jumped off the bike and strode up to Julie's front door. He rang the bell, knocked loudly and at the same time yelled, 'Ollie!! Are you in there?!'

Tony wondered what was going on but did not want Kurt to see him there or ask him any questions. He drove quietly away while Kurt was still occupied with trying to get a response from the house.

Chapter 9

That evening Tony made his way to the Dog in the Pond where he had arranged to meet Kurt and Jambo. Just before he reached the pub he happened to glance down a side footpath and saw a young guy climbing up on to the roof of the pub. He had a cable slung over his shoulder attached to a small electronic box and short aerial.

Tony grinned. He knew exactly who it was and what he was up to. Not making a sound, Tony crept to the bottom of the wall. From there he could see the other end of the cable running across to an old Luton box van parked in the shadows out of sight. It was painted a deep purple with an air-brushed mural depicting a towering black freedom fighter astride what seemed to be national grid power lines which had been pulled up from the roots and crushed in one of the figure's hands. The figure's other hand held a radio antenna with emanating radio waves which formed the logo: Free Radio, Bazz FM, Britain's Loudest. Smiling to himself, Tony tugged gently on the cable and called in a deepened voice, 'O.K. Laddie . . . You're nicked!'

The guy on the pub roof went into immediate shock. He froze and nearly lost his grip, just managing to hang on and save himself from falling. This was not what Tony had meant to happen. It was not even Bazz himself, but a guy who sometimes helped out. 'Sorry,' Tony muttered, backing away as he decided it would be better not to be there.

Opening the door to the pub, Tony heard the unmistakable rhythm of Jungle-Rap – the volume at something like number eight. The music was coming from a mobile sound desk with a turntable, cassette decks and speaker towers – everything that went to make up a DJ sound and light show. Amongst this, Bazz was setting up his Bazz FM backdrop. When this was done, Bazz pulled a cable similar to the one coming from his van across to his sound desk. He plugged it into a small black box with a large rocker switch labelled 'Off – Transmit'.

There was no sign of either Kurt or Jambo but as Tony reached the bar, the pub door burst open. Kurt dashed in and whistled across to Bazz before tossing his 'Flying Virgin' helmet over the heads of the crowd. Bazz caught the helmet neatly and dropped it into an open flight case, threw in a couple of loops of cable and shut the lid. Kurt ducked low into the crowd. He worked his way to the bar, peeling off his leather jacket as he went and wrapping it around a girl's shoulders as he passed. He borrowed a glass from someone else and then surfaced at the bar, immediately adopting a nonchalant pose that indicated he had been there all evening.

Two uniformed police officers appeared in the doorway. Bazz hid the transmitter switch down out of sight and hit the master fader on the desk to pump the volume up past eleven. The policemen took one look around and, realizing it was a complete waste of their time and the taxpayers' money, they left. Kurt grinned, returned the glass to its owner and retrieved his jacket. He waved to Bazz in thanks and, catching sight of Tony, wound his way across to him.

Tony shook his head at him, shouting above the music, 'That helmet's trouble.'

'Make's life . . . interesting as well as thirsty,' Kurt said. Tony took the hint and turned to the bar.

Kurt's attention was caught by what appeared to be an animated row going on over at the sound desk. Kurt wandered across. Natasha's father, Greg, was pointing repeatedly at Bazz, his gear and the door. It was hard to hear but it was obvious that Greg was unhappy about the sound level. Bazz was protesting. 'These people like loud music, that's what I do.' He pointed at the writing on his sign proclaiming 'Britain's Loudest'. 'You booked me, man,' he argued. 'You going back on the deal?'

Greg nodded. 'Yes. It's too much. Now get

this lot packed up and out . . . now.'

Realizing what was happening, Kurt whistled across to Bazz. He then pointed to his ears and gestured for Bazz to take the volume down. Bazz looked at Kurt, then at Greg and back at Kurt who mouthed 'Now'. Bazz pulled the fader back to eight. Kurt nodded.

'See,' Bazz said to Greg. 'Give the people what they want.'

'Thanks for that,' Greg smiled at Kurt. Bazz turned away to retrieve his transmit switch, 'What's that?' Greg asked suspiciously.

Kurt stepped in again and said dismissively, 'It's just an effects gizmo. He'll keep it down now, Mr. Andersen.'

Greg looked at Kurt again and recognized him as the guy he had found on his doorstep the other night after Louise's party.

'Bazz gets a bit er . . . temperamental. Likes to stand on his artistic integrity,' Kurt continued.

'Another minute and he'd have been out – sitting on his artistic backside,' Greg was smiling now. 'What are you drinking?'

'That's very nice of you Mr. Andersen,' Kurt grinned.

'Greg,' said Greg, holding out his hand. Kurt shook it. He did not always get on quite so well with girls' fathers.

Tony, who had been watching, caught up with Kurt sitting down at a free table next to a window. He slapped him on the shoulder.

'Got your feet under the table there,' he joked. 'It's a pity you're not as popular with his daughter.'

Natasha was upstairs in her bedroom getting ready. Her room was the female equivalent of Kurt's in terms of tidiness. It was fairly large and had originally been neatly laid out with a futon bed, chair, bentwood coat stand, a long run of wardrobes along one wall and a full length worktop with drawers and cupboards which formed a dressing table and study area along the window wall. The frame of the dressing-table mirror was covered with souvenirs – photo booth shots of Natasha with various friends, gig tickets, American sweet wrappers and a large photo of a border collie leaping to retrieve a rubber bone thrown by what looked like a ten-year-old Natasha. As in Kurt's room, the walls were almost completely obscured by mementoes and were a record of the developing stages of Natasha's life. There were framed school sports certificates, a lacrosse stick, a Planet Hollywood poster and various posters of Keanu Reeves, Brad Pitt and Kurt Cobain who was also one of Kurt's heroes. There was a massive collage of family photographs including black and white prints of her mother's and father's early lives. Another section of the wall near the window was covered with her own poetic thoughts and messages from friends. The coat stand sagged under the weight of various clothes and bags and seemed to be under siege from the vast army of shoes and boots amassed around it. The worktop was littered with make-up and other cosmetics as well as many books and folders from college. The study area was flanked on one side by a TV and CD mini system and a Packard-Bell PC with a collection of teddies crawling over it. The room was particularly chaotic tonight, with the floor littered with clothes that had not made it through the selection process.

Natasha was applying the last layer of lip gloss at her mirror while Dawn leaned back among the collection of cushions on the bed. She turned over one of the lace and silk cushions which was in fact a pyjama case with Natasha's name embroidered on it.

'How long did it take your Aunt to make that?' she asked.

'Eight years.'

'Persistent.'

'I really wanted it when I was ten,' said Natasha, smiling at the thought. 'You staying over tonight?'

'No. I promised Cindy and Max I'd get back, just in case . . .'

'Has Terry ever tried anything with Cindy?' Natasha asked, seriously.

Dawn shook her head and shuddered. 'But when he's had a drink, who knows . . . Anyway, she's got my number,' she held up her mobile phone and changed the subject. 'Do you think we should check to see if Louise is all right?

She's been in the loo a long time.'

'I've already made a prize idiot of myself once today,' said Natasha.

'It has been forty-five minutes. I'll go,' Dawn made for the door just as it opened. Dawn leapt backwards on to the cushions and grabbed a magazine from the pile near the bed. In the tension, Natasha's lip brush slipped and smudged on her cheek. Louise didn't notice. She was too busy holding a tissue to her eyes and nose, the evidence of another sob session, with red eyes to prove it. While Natasha and Dawn were dressed for a night out, Louise was swathed in androgynous layers.

Seeing their looks, Louise said huffily, 'I'm still alive if that's what's worrying you.'

She began picking up Natasha's clothes, folding them and stacking them on the end of the futon. 'How could you even think I'd kill myself.'

'Louise, please!' beseeched Natasha. 'I've said I'm sorry. And can you stop acting like my mother. Leave my clothes.'

Louise started to sob again. 'That's my trouble. People always walk all over me.'

'I only asked you to stop . . .' Natasha was exasperated. She pointed to her overflowing laundry basket. 'You can sort that lot out if you like.'

Dawn pulled a frantic 'shut up you're making it worse' face. Natasha answered with a 'well I don't know what to do', face and went back to her make-up repair.

'Come on, Lou. He was a rat. There'll be plenty more in the sewers,' Dawn tried, ignoring Natasha's incredulous face in the mirror.

'I don't want anyone else. I love Joe,' Louise was the romantic heroine again. 'He meant everything to me. We were compatible birth signs and everything. That's why I gave myself to him.'

Dawn looked surprised and horrified. Natasha's make-up brush slipped again. They tried to question her about exactly what she meant. 'You *gave* yourself to him?!'

'Totally,' said Louise who was lost in her suffering heroine role, trying to look pale and tragic.

'Why did I let you talk me into that!?' Greg asked Natasha, pointing to Bazz, when the three girls came down to the bar.

'He's brilliant,' Natasha smiled, knowing her dad was only too happy to do anything that encouraged Natasha and her friends to stay at the pub – where he could see his daughter was safe.

'Loud,' Greg retorted.

'Britain's loudest,' Dawn added.

'He was nearly "Britain's sorest head" too, until your mate stepped in – Kurt. Nice guy,' Greg grinned, sorting out Kurt's drink.

Natasha grimaced not altogether fooling Dawn. 'He's quite passable isn't he?' Dawn asked, watching for Natasha's reaction.

Natasha was suspiciously evasive, 'That depends on whether you're masochistic or not,' she answered.

Louise was standing nearby looking miserable. 'What are we going to do now,' she asked.

'Enjoy ourselves?' Natasha suggested.

This was too much for Louise. 'That's easy for you two. Your lives aren't over. You don't know how I feel, what condition I'm in. I'm going to the loo.'

'Again!?' Dawn could not help herself enquiring.

'Do you want me to cry in public?' Louise said coldly. Dawn began to go with her. 'Don't worry. I'm not going to kill myself.'

Dawn sighed with frustration. There was no helping some people. Perhaps Louise enjoyed being miserable, the drama and attention.

It was now Natasha's turn to be concerned. 'What did she mean, we don't know what "condition" she's in?'

'Mentally I suppose,' Dawn shrugged.'

'But suppose . . . physically? Where did she go this morning?' Natasha paused, before answering herself. 'The doctor's. Gave herself to him she said. "Condition"?' Natasha did not need to say more. The look on Dawn's face showed she had reached the same conclusion and the pair rushed off to find Louise.

By now Jambo had also arrived, using his usual means of entry. First he had surprised a couple having a quiet drink when his head suddenly popped through the window next to where they were sitting. Having located Tony and Kurt he then appeared outside their window. Tony unlocked it and Jambo jumped down on to the bench next to them, wearing his favourite Chaos Theory T-shirt and helping himself to one of the full bottles on the table. 'What's that?' he asked, nodding at the letter Tony was reading. 'It's from my insurance company,' Kurt said. 'They won't pay the full value of the car.'

'I could have told you that,' Jambo was off on one of his favourite themes. 'It's all a con. Like all big businesses, all they want is your cash. Once they've got that, they deliver the small print.'

Kurt shrugged philosophically. 'There's not a lot I can do except move on – and kill my brother.'

'I'd have ripped his head off by now,' said Jambo.

'He wasn't in when I got the letter,' Kurt explained. 'I even went round to his girlfriend's house,' Tony shifted uncomfortably. 'Anyway if I'd caught up with him then I might have been on the ten o'clock news tonight.' Kurt made a strangling gesture and at the same time noticed Natasha and Dawn hurry into the bar. Kurt quickly stood up and walked off in their direction.

'I'll have a tin,' Jambo shouted after him. He turned to Tony when Kurt was out of earshot.

'Mr Benson seems smitten, wouldn't you say Hutchinson old chap?'

'Harry Met Sally,' Tony twisted his head to get a better view of Jambo's copy of *More* magazine.

At first Dawn and Natasha were too preoccupied to notice Kurt standing just behind them at the bar.

'Why didn't you say something?' Dawn asked.

'I couldn't. Not after the suicide business,' Natasha squirmed at the memory.

'If you think she's pregnant, you should . . .' Dawn began.

'Not just me,' Natasha jumped in. 'You think she is too.'

'Well we won't know unless we ask,' Dawn was about to carry on when she spotted Kurt. He had his back to them but was obviously leaning back to catch every word. Sensing the conversation had stopped, Kurt turned in mock surprise.

'Get lost, Benson,' said Natasha, coldly.

'Don't take out your angst on me. I didn't contribute to your friend's "condition",' Kurt played the wide-eyed innocent. Natasha felt guilty that he had overheard their comments, 'May I say that you two are looking, er . . . well, er . . .'

'Well what?' asked Dawn, impatiently.

'Er . . . well . . . "well",' Kurt grinned. Then in answer to Natasha's look he added, 'Hey. I'm just trying to minimize the scope for rejection here.' This at least made Dawn smile. Natasha ignored it as she saw Louise emerge.

Louise looked depressed and headed for the door, stopping close to where Kurt was quietly telling Tony and Jambo what he had just overheard. 'I think I'll go home,' she told Natasha and Dawn.

Dawn tried to persuade her to stay. 'You might as well be miserable in company.'

'You could stay over here if you don't feel too good,' Natasha backed her up.

'I feel fine. I'm not ill or anything . . .' Louise stopped, seeing the expressions on her friends' faces and also those of the three guys who looked quickly away. 'What? What is it? What's going on?' she asked, suspiciously.

Natasha looked sheepish, took a deep breath and after an encouraging look from Dawn asked quietly, 'What did you mean when you talked about your "condition"?'

Louise seemed completely puzzled until Jambo decided he could bear the suspense no longer. He leaned over between them. 'She means,' he said. 'Are you up the spout?'

Everyone froze and hoped the ground would swallow them up. All except Jambo who appeared to be completely unaware of the effect his honesty had caused. Louise was outraged.

'How dare you?' she exploded, first at Jambo and then at Natasha and Dawn. 'First you think I'm about to kill myself, now you think I'm pregnant. What kind of idiot do you think I am?' she was about to leave when she saw Jambo's magazine. 'And what sort of magazines do you read?' Louise gave everyone a look of utter contempt and swept out.

Dawn and Natasha ran after her, not sure exactly how they were to make amends. Natasha turned back at the door. There was something she had to do first. She walked back to Jambo and kicked him hard on the shin. Kurt started to laugh but not for long. Natasha glared and, realizing he must have told Jambo, picked up a drink to throw at him. Kurt saw it coming and ducked, leaving Tony to take the hit. This made Jambo roar with laughter. Natasha groaned with exasperation and hurried after Dawn.

Chapter 10

The next morning cleaning was underway at the Dog in the Pond. Greg was surprised to see Natasha appear, unusually early and having made more effort with her appearance than normal for college.

'Get on to the Guiness Book of Records quickly,' he called to the cleaner. 'Nat's been up early three times this week,' then he turned to Natasha, grinning. 'So who is it then?'

'Who is who?' Natasha smiled, innocently, not fooling Greg. She was about to leave for college when Greg picked up an envelope.

'Did you get them?' she asked, excitedly.

'Yes. Although I don't know what you need to bother going to see this lot for . . . drag out my old Kinks and Small Faces L.P.s . . .' Greg said. 'Sorry – vinyl. And if you want Oasis, just listen to the Beatles.'

Natasha listened patiently. She had heard it all before.

'I know,' she answered, then pointed at his Pink Floyd Pulse T-shirt. 'And if you hang on to anything long enough it'll eventually come back into fashion.'

Natasha left her father chuckling and walked to the bus stop, giving a last hopeful look around for a familiar figure on a motorbike, before boarding her bus.

Kurt was still asleep, despite the insistently bleeping electronic alarm.

Eventually an arm slid out from under the duvet, fumbled around for the clock and killed the sound. Daylight was slanting in through the closed slats of the wooden blind and in the semi-darkness, the room had a definite 'morning after' appearance. Seconds later, the silence was again shattered by a loud, ringing bell as another alarm clock began a second-wave attack. This was silenced almost immediately by another arm – this time from the other side of the duvet. The duvet dwellers slumbered on until . . . the bedroom door slowly opened and Ollie, dressed for school, tiptoed in. He found the TV remote control on his way to the window. He took a firm grip on the Venetian-blind cord and with one swift and practised movement, he yanked up the blind and hit the remote control. The room flooded with sunlight and sound. Ollie then bounded across to the door, pulling it shut behind him just in time to avoid the boot that Kurt lobbed at his head.

'Mum told me to wake you up,' Ollie's head popped round the door and disappeared quickly. He slammed the door and heard a second boot thud against it.

The person under the other side of the duvet stirred as Kurt switched off the TV and flopped back into bed. He was about to slip into oblivion when the forces of daylight launched the ultimate weapon . . . Kurt's mother, Juliet.

'What died in here recently?' she asked, pulling a face.

'O.K. I just want to mellow out today,' Kurt sighed, sitting upright, waiting for the onslaught.

'I'm not concerned about you,' his mother said. 'But if James doesn't want to "mellow out" of his job, he should get up now!'

Jambo's head appeared and squinted at the clock. Then his adrenalin took over, he was late. He stood up, realized he was dressed only in boxer shorts and grabbed the duvet.

'It's all right, James,' Juliet said. 'I've seen it all before.'

'Not mine, Mrs B,' grinned Jambo, his normal self again.

'True,' she pondered. 'And even I couldn't face that at this time of the morning.' Juliet was about to go, but first warned Kurt, 'I'll be out till lunch time, so you can "mellow out" until then. After that I'm coming in here to disinfect the place before the Environmental Health people quarantine us all.'

Kurt groaned and Jambo laughed, pulling on his clothes and disappearing through the window.

Tony was already awake and out, trying to see Julie. He slowed as he passed the end of her street. He paused for a moment and then thought better of it. He could not simply knock at her door and ask her out, especially not at eight-fifteen in the morning. He decided on a different approach. He would carry on and catch her a little later on her way to school, as if he had run into her by chance.

He waited outside a corner newsagents close to school and ten minutes later saw Julie in the distance walking in his direction. Tony hurried into the shop and bought a copy of *Motor Cycle News*. He then hovered near the door waiting for his big moment to step out and 'casually' bump into her. But Julie was taking her time and Tony felt uncomfortably aware of the fact that he was hovering. Noticing the slightly suspicious looks the owner was giving him, he started to flick through the magazines again. He was still preoccupied with glancing outside and felt a complete idiot when two young schoolboys sniggered at him because he was actually holding a copy of *Caravan World*. Feeling any 'cool' he possessed fast evaporating, he left the shop and tried to fix his hair in his motorbike mirror.

'Right Tony,' Tony said to himself. 'This is it. She must be nearly at the shop now.'

Tony took a deep breath and stepped confidently around the corner to meet Julie. But there was no one there. The pavement was empty. He looked in all directions and finally spotted her, climbing into the Cunningham Driving School car, chatting away to her mate.

Feeling totally deflated, Tony climbed back on to his bike and drove off towards college and work. He arrived at the same time as Natasha. She waved and hurried to catch up with Louise.

'Hi, Lou,' Natasha greeted her. 'How are you feeling today?'

'Crushed, rejected, lonely . . .' she walked on leaving Natasha who raised her eyes to the sky, thinking 'Here we go again.'

Natasha followed Louise into the lavatories. Several of the cubicle doors were shut.

'Louise?' she called tentatively.

'Go away and leave me alone,' came the reply. At least Natasha knew which cubicle Louise was in. She went into the one next to it, climbed up on the cistern and looked down at Louise, who was sitting on the seat lid, just 'wanting to be alone'.

'C'mon Lou . . . Joe isn't worth all this. In fact, no guy is worth all this,' Natasha tried to reason.

'Well how about your friends thinking you're a lunatic, or a slut?'

Natasha had to admit that Louise had a point there, but then again, 'What were we supposed to think?'

'You thought I'd really commit suicide and that I was pregnant?!? I can't believe you,' Louise said angrily.

'We-e-ll based on what we knew . . .' it had seemed reasonable at the time, Natasha thought.

'You knew me!' and with that Louise stormed out, passing two girls on their way in. They looked curiously at Natasha still perched on the cistern, hanging over into the next cubicle. She smiled sheepishly and jumped down. She quickly left to begin wandering the corridors searching for Louise. She supposed Louise was right. Knowing her they should not have jumped to the conclusions they had. The trouble was, Joe was Louise's first 'serious' boyfriend and she did take a romantic view of life. Before starting sixth-form college, where she had met Natasha, she had gone to a private girls' school and as her parents' only daughter and the middle child, she had been very protected.

It had taken a great deal of persuading for her to be allowed to attend the college. Now as far as her parents were concerned she was at college because she 'didn't enjoy the culture of her private school and therefore never reached her full potential'. For Louise the answer was more simple – her GCSE grades were not good enough for Lady Mountington's sixth form and, as she saw it, she just did not have the ability to carry on with Latin and economics as the entry to a degree in either law or architecture. Her mother was a solicitor and her father an architect and these subjects represented her parents' hopes for her rather than a personal goal. The truth was Louise lacked the motivation for what she termed a 'boring professional career' and she was now taking a course in English and Theatre Studies at college having always wanted to try drama. And there had certainly been plenty of that in the last few days.

Finally, Natasha caught up with her. 'Louise! I'm sorry. Dawn's sorry . . . We're all sorry. I know it's bad, but don't make it worse. Joe would really have won then.'

'It's not a question of winning and losing. It's about emotions, self-respect and loyalty!' Louise spoke pointedly.

'I've said I'm sorry, what do you want me to do? Kill myself? Oh no! Wrong thing to say.'

Louise gave her a withering look but seemed to calm down. 'I know it's not your fault. It's not even Joe's fault.' Natasha was puzzled. Louise continued. 'It was all in the stars, the Christmas Edition Year Ahead Section,' she pulled out a tattered piece of paper and began to read, ' "This is going to be a momentous year . . . When you learn the real feelings of love: good and bad".' This was another of Louise's interests – astrology, the stars, in fact anything supernatural.

Perhaps her stars will say something good soon. Maybe that will convince her to stop moping,' Natasha thought to herself on her way to her first class.

Chapter 11

At lunchtime Kurt vacated his room ready for his mother's blitz. He hoped she might have forgotten and if he was also out of the way, there would be nothing to remind her. Anyway, he had unfinished business with Ollie. Kurt planned to catch his brother off-guard when Ollie would be least expecting to see him. With this in mind, Kurt pulled up outside Ollie's school. There were groups of pupils milling around, going in and out on their lunch breaks but Kurt quickly spotted Ollie. He was trying to talk to Julie who did not look at all pleased to see him. Ollie did not look pleased to see Kurt and tried to make a run for the school gate. Kurt was too quick and slid the bike round to block his path. He thrust the spare helmet he had been carrying at his brother.

'Get on,' he snapped, pushing Ollie towards the back of the bike. Ollie realized there was little point arguing. The bike roared away to the mystified stares of Ollie's gang and the admiring looks of Julie and her friends.

Kurt took them to the town centre and

stopped outside a building society. Ollie got off the bike but still did not know what was going on.

'What's all this about dog breath?' Ollie asked.

'Make it payable to me,' Kurt slapped Ollie's building society account book into his brother's palm.

'All my money?' Ollie realized this was exactly what Kurt wanted. 'No way man.'

'It's only half the amount it will cost me to fix my car – which you totalled,' Ollie looked as if he was about to argue but Kurt continued, 'Don't even think about complaining. Let's see, what are you guilty of? Driving without a licence, driving without insurance, driving a car without permission. Do you want me to go on?'

'O.K.' Ollie knew when he was beaten. 'But what am I going to do if Mum and Dad find out all my money's gone?'

'Who cares. You choose. Who can you handle best? Them? Or me? And don't forget there is also the little matter of what they might do if they had the merest hint of what really happened to the car,' Kurt didn't need to say more. Ollie sighed and walked into the building society.

Kurt had been waiting a couple of minutes when he saw a police car turn the corner at the end of the street. He was caught between making a dash for it or waiting for Ollie and his cash. He quickly realized he wouldn't be able to get the bike fired up and away in time and, deciding that discretion was the better part of not getting nicked, he picked up his two helmets and sauntered away as casually as he could. He stood out of sight, watching. The police car was about to pass when the driver noticed Kurt's bike. As usual it had no licence plate or tax disc. Kurt grabbed Ollie on his way out of the building society and whispered a plan to him. Ollie looked horrified.

'No way!' he exclaimed.

'Just do it!' Kurt glared. Ollie started to go but not before Kurt had removed his building society passbook and cheque. Kurt stepped back to watch. He looked apprehensive. The policeman was talking on his radio and examining the bike frame, trying to get a number. Ollie was hesitating nervously. Kurt gestured for him to 'get on with it', whereupon Ollie took a deep breath and ran into a clothes shop, emerging seconds later with two jackets on hangers. They were security tagged and as soon as Ollie ran out of the shop, the alarm sounded. Ollie threw the jackets back into the shop and raced around the corner. The noise of the alarm had the desired effect upon the policeman. He saw the shop assistants at the door and what appeared to be a thief running away. He turned his back on the bike and took off in pursuit.

Kurt grinned, pulled on his helmet and jumped on to the bike. He kick-started it and roared off. Ollie was halfway down the alley with the policeman turning in behind him when Kurt appeared at the end waiting for Ollie to scramble on. They roared off, leaving the policeman behind staring after them.

Ollie was only too pleased to jump down off the bike when Kurt dropped him at school.

'You're crazy,' Ollie exploded. 'Absolutely mental . . . insane. Do you know that?'

Kurt nodded.

'It's not funny, Kurt. It's . . .'

'Irresponsible?' Kurt finished. 'Like you taking my car, without my permission and nearly killing your girlfriend's best mate? That kind of irresponsible?' Ollie knew he had no answer to that. Kurt held on to Ollie's arm and decided to act the big brother and make sure the lesson had been learned. 'Tell me. Will you ever do anything like that again?'

'Get off,' Ollie tried to pull free.

'Will you?'

'No.'

'Now that's responsible.'

Chapter 12

Natasha waited in vain for Louise to meet her for lunch. She set off to look for her and finally found her in a small tutorial room, staring out of the window. Louise appeared to be lost in thought, and fighting back tears. Natasha was at a loss about what to say. She wondered again how long Louise would keep this up for and what could be done to bring her back to her senses. What Natasha actually said was, 'I've been waiting for you downstairs to go for lunch,' which succeeded in causing Louise to give up the fight against tears and flee. Natasha followed her to the college toilets where Louise had again hidden herself in the same cubicle as before. She quickly emerged dabbing her eyes.

'Don't tell me about fish in the sea, that life must go on, or that he's not worth it. I know all that. I just need help – to grieve,' Louise announced.

Natasha nodded. This seemed quite positive, a good sign in fact. 'Do you want to do it alone?' she asked more than a little hopefully.

'A shoulder to cry on might be useful,'

Natasha turned hers towards Louise which at least made her smile briefly. Louise took a deep breath. 'I need to face the world,' and she swept out. Natasha was rather impressed.

'Facing the world' began in the college canteen, or more specifically, the queue at the counter. Lewis Richardson, president of his own appreciation society, had decided it was Natasha's lucky week. He was standing in the queue in front of her. Smiling oilily, he fished out a swatch of tickets from his shirt pocket.

'I thought you might want tickets for Ragmoor Park – Oasis *and* Blur?' he said.

'The price would be too high,' Natasha smiled brightly.

'Who said anything about paying . . .'

'I'd have to go with you?' She thought, what a creep!

'We--e-ll, that was the idea,' Lewis said.

'As I thought. The price is far too high,' Natasha smiled even more brightly and stepped past to the cashier.

The queue sniggered as Lewis noticeably deflated. But to Natasha's horror Lewis turned to Louise. 'Ah well. At least you and I know how to handle rejection, eh Louise?'

Louise looked at him for a moment, dropped her tray and rushed out, leaving Lewis and the lunch queue shocked and stunned. Natasha picked up her own tray and ran after her. At least she knew where Louise was going. The two girls who had seen her standing on the cistern smiled quizzically at her on their way out as Natasha hurried into the toilets with her lunch tray. This time she did not hang about.

She slid the tray under Louise's cubicle door. 'If you can't face the world, at least eat something.'

At the end of lunch hour Louise was out of her cubicle again talking to Natasha who was still trying to lift her spirits.

'Do you think I should have slept with Joe?' Louise asked. 'If I had, perhaps he wouldn't have gone off with "that girl".'

'He would have,' Natasha was scathing. 'After he'd got what he wanted.'

'I'll have to do it sometime.'

'But not with Joe,' Natasha pulled a face.

'He was the only serious boyfriend I've ever had,' Louise looked wistful. 'It's easy for you. You never have any trouble.'

'Oh please! Lou, you'll be fine. You're great. There's plenty more . . .'

'Don't say it!' Louise butted in. 'Anyway, you've only got to look at yourself and then at me to see which of us any guy would prefer.'

'I'm late, I've got to go. I'll meet you back here,' Natasha watched Louise slope away. She did not know what else she could do.

In the canteen, Lewis Richardson was again trying his luck. This time with Tony and with a rather different aim. He caught Tony's attention by asking, 'Any chance of sneaking a couple of women through the kitchen on Saturday night?'

Tony liked Lewis about as much as Natasha did. He nodded. 'Two chances: fat chance and no chance. That's why they introduced ID checks – to stop people like you sneaking anyone in.'

'Oh c'mon. I can't get them in otherwise and I'm that close with one of them,' Lewis held his thumb and forefinger a centimetre apart.

'Yeah! That's about the size of it,' Tony laughed.

'Listen mate,' Lewis tried a different approach. 'I'll give you Ragmoor Park tickets at face value. I could get three times the price for them.'

'Got mine. And my ID for Saturday night,' Tony went off smiling, to find Kurt waiting for him in the kitchen.

'Ollie coughed up for the car,' Kurt said.

'I never thought he'd volunteer to do that,' Tony was impressed. Kurt laughed and waved Ollie's building society book at him. 'Neither did he. But I've still got to raise the other half of the money and there's no way the car will be ready in time for Ragmoor Park.'

'We'll get there somehow. They're selling tickets in here for three times the face value,' Tony said. 'You've got our tickets safe haven't you?'

Kurt patted his shirt pocket and realized he was wearing a T-shirt. Muttering something about a 'red shirt' and looking distinctly pale, Kurt rushed outside to his bike and roared off. Twenty minutes later, he rushed into his room. He did a double take. Was it his room? His mother was just finishing. The room was tidily transformed.

'I did warn you,' Mrs Benson said in answer to Kurt's shocked face.

'Where is it?' Kurt was trying not to panic. 'My red shirt . . .' Downstairs, the washing machine hummed. Kurt covered his face with his hands. 'Tell me you didn't.'

Chapter 13

After Kurt had dropped him back at school, Ollie's day had not improved. His marks had been consistently bad in every lesson that afternoon and now Julie was trying to finish with him.

'It's over,' she said, coldly.

'What?!' Ollie could not believe it.

'O-V-E-R. Over. Finished. We are no longer an item,' Julie wanted to make sure he understood.

'You mean just like that?' Ollie did not want to believe it.

'Since the car business.'

Ollie groaned. 'I've had all this from Kurt. He made me give him all my money this morning. I've paid my debt to society, big style. So why?' As far as Ollie was concerned this was only the slightest exaggeration.

'Isn't nearly killing me, and Sarah, enough?'

'Why now? Why didn't you say then?' Ollie was genuinely confused and he did really like Julie.

'I must have been in trauma,' Julie's mind

was made up. She went home.

Tony waited, leaning against his bike, in Julie's now familiar street. He was determined not to repeat that morning's fiasco. When he saw Julie come into view he began to walk to meet her. It was now or never . . . or perhaps not. Tony's nerve failed him and he ducked out of sight behind a van. Realizing he was making more of a fool of himself by hiding than he would by asking her out and risking rejection, Tony stepped out from behind the van. Julie was opening her door. He was about to miss her again.

Panicking and not stopping to think what he was doing, Tony hurried forward and shouted, 'Stop! Wait!' the words died on his lips as Julie turned and looked at him.

He stammered incoherently.

'You're Ollie's brother's mate,' Julie said, recognizing him. 'I've seen you with him.'

Tony continued burbling, ending with, 'Tony . . . that's me . . . Kurt's mate.'

Julie looked bewildered but was beginning to smile. 'Have you seen *Four Weddings and a Funeral*?' Tony nodded. 'Is this the scene where he wants to marry her?'

This plunged Tony into even greater confusion. 'Marry?! Er . . . no . . . I . . . er . . .'

By now Julie was laughing. 'Do you want to ask me out?'

'No! I mean . . . yes . . . yes that's it.'

'What about Ollie?' Julie asked.

Tony looked sheepish. 'What about him?'

'I've finished with him. And yes. I would like to go out with you,' Julie smiled.

Tony smiled back, hardly believing his ears.

Ollie would have liked not to believe his eyes. He had followed Julie home, wanting to find out more about why she had dumped him, hoping to change her mind. He watched her talking to Tony and felt his eyes begin to mist. He rubbed them briskly and walked away before anyone noticed him.

Kurt was playing a Muddy Waters blues riff on his Stratocaster at high volume when suddenly a hand dropped on his shoulder. He jumped and turned to see Tony, grinning.

'Your mother let me in.'

'Who needs a mother like mine,' Kurt spoke bitterly but even he noticed how happy Tony looked.

'Do you know what life's all about?' Tony asked.

'You mean there's a greater purpose to life than getting laid?'

'Relationships . . .'

'It is just about getting laid then?' Kurt took another look at Tony. 'Have you just got laid?'

At this point Ollie burst in, took one look at Tony and flew at him. 'I'll kill him!'

'Why?' Kurt held onto Ollie.

'Ask him.'

Kurt turned to Tony, who looked embarrassed, and back to Ollie. Kurt was puzzled.

'Julie dumped me. For him!'

'Is this true?' Kurt looked stern.

'I saw you,' Ollie yelled.

'Well?' asked Kurt.

'I asked her out,' Tony spoke defensively. 'She told me she'd dumped him.'

Tony looked sheepish and felt like a rat. Ollie looked angry and vindicated. Kurt looked stern and then grinned.

'Way to go, Tone!' Kurt said.

Ollie tried to lunge at Tony but Kurt grabbed him and frog-marched him to the door.

'It's been a valuable day for you, Ollie. First you learn about responsibility and then the fickleness of women . . . and just because you tried to kill her.'

Ollie recognized the truth of this for long enough for Kurt to shove him out through the door. Kurt turned back to grin at Tony until he laughed with embarrassment.

Ollie's head appeared around the door. 'I'm glad Mum put your tickets in the wash.' He disappeared leaving Kurt to face Tony.

'Tell me it's not the Ragmoor tickets,' Tony pleaded. 'I've had one of the best days of my life. Tell me it isn't about to crumble around me.'

At this point, the window opened and Jambo climbed through.

'All right, men?' he sensed something was wrong.

'Is it true Kurt?' Tony asked. 'What's happened to the tickets, Kurt?' he insisted.

Kurt picked up the washed and matted remains of the tickets. Tony looked at them in disbelief. Jambo also appeared to be in shock. They both stared at Kurt. How could he have let this happen?

'Look at the room,' Kurt gestured around him. 'There's been the disaster of all mothers in here.'

'You left the Ragmoor tickets in your pocket?' Jambo looked at him in disbelief.

'She never cleans up, man,' Kurt tried to explain. 'O.K. You look after the tickets from now on.' He could not bear the accusing expressions on Tony's and Jambo's faces. 'Look guys. I admit it. Whether I like it or not my mother is my responsibility. And as such, I will get us some more tickets.'

'How?!'

That was the big question. The concert had been sold out for months.

'You told me they were selling them at college,' Kurt began.

'For three times the value.'

'No way,' Jambo was adamant. 'You faked those invites for Louise's party.'

'A concert ticket is just a little bit more tricky.'

Tony grinned, 'Not tickets. All we need is one dork, with tickets, who will swap them for a college ID card. A dork that needs to impress his girlfriend because he's only this far from being laid.'

'That kind of dork would be good,' Kurt nodded.

'All we need is to borrow an ID,' Tony grinned. 'Who do we know at college who has one?'

Half an hour later, Natasha was getting ready to go out and trying to convince Louise that she wanted to go too. There was a knock at the door and Greg appeared.

'There's someone to see you in the pub,' he said.

Kurt, Jambo and Tony waited in the bar until Natasha appeared. She looked curiously at the three of them, wondering what they were up to.

'Hi, Natasha,' Kurt smiled. 'Look . . .'

'No,' whatever they were up to, Natasha did not want any part in it. She disappeared back upstairs.

'Can I borrow that technique at some stage?' Jambo asked. They were about to go when Julie arrived to see Sarah. She broke into a rather silly grin when she saw Tony, matched by his equally soppy expression. Noticing Kurt, she turned to go – she felt embarrassed and guilty about Ollie. But Kurt had another plan.

'Julie!' he called her back. 'Good call on our Ollie. He's an idiot.'

Kurt whispered something to Tony and pushed him forward. Jambo looked puzzled.

'I think for all our sakes they should be alone,' he said, grinning. Slowly it dawned on Jambo. Julie was best friends with Sarah,

Natasha's sister and knew Natasha well . . .

The next morning, Kurt's room looked as if it had been under assault. There were again two bodies under a mound of bedding but as the alarm began its electronic beep, Kurt was already sitting yawning at his computer, surrounded by screwed up twists of paper. Finally satisfied with the image being printed, he pulled up the blinds and turned to the groaning lumps stirring in the bed. He waved a sheet of college ID cards in front of their bleary eyes.

'We are in business!'

At nine o'clock, with the ID cards now in plastic covers, Tony and Kurt were in college talking to Lewis, who seemed hesitant.

Kurt pulled his own card from his pocket. 'It gets me in and out – no problem. All you need is a photo booth photo, signature and your girlfriend's in, anytime,' Kurt was persuasive. 'What have you got to lose? I'm giving you full value on the tickets.'

'But they're worth more money . . .' Lewis still hesitated.

'How far away from being laid is he?' Kurt asked. Tony held up his finger and thumb and grinned at Lewis. This seemed to swing the deal. Lewis took a final look at the IDs and held out the tickets.

That was when Natasha and Louise appeared. 'What are you doing here, Benson?'

'Just a bit of Christian kindness, helping out

someone who's in trouble . . . or who wants to get himself in trouble,' Kurt was feeling confident now.

Lewis did not appreciate the joke. Natasha pulled a memo from the notice board and held it out to Lewis. The effect was dramatic. He grabbed his tickets from Kurt and thrust the IDs and money back into his hand. He stomped off.

Kurt grabbed the notice and began to read. 'They're changing the design of the college ID card? What?!'

'As from tomorrow,' Natasha elaborated. 'Too many fakes in circulation!'

She smiled sweetly. Tony expected Kurt to be angry but he grinned back. He knew he had been set up.

'So why didn't you say something last night?' he asked.

'If you will get Tony to talk to Julie, to talk to Sarah, to talk to me – what do you expect?' Natasha was still smiling. Kurt guessed there was something else.

'You wouldn't know of anywhere we can get tickets would you? Not just for me . . . but for Tony and Jambo?' Kurt quizzed.

'Well,' Natasha grinned, enjoying the tease. 'For Tony's and Jambo's sakes, perhaps. But the price might be too high,' Kurt looked just a little deflated. She waved her envelope at him. 'You might have to go with me!' With that she left for her first class. Kurt turned to Tony.

'Was that real, or am I having an out-of-body experience?'

'Real – unless I'm having the same dream.'

Kurt grinned broadly watching Natasha walk away. She looked back over her shoulder at him and smiled.

Chapter 14

Another day and again the alarm sounded in Kurt's bedroom. The sole occupant silenced the alarm and looked around for Kurt. It was Jambo. He often ended up staying over at Kurt's house. He lived with his mother in a house that was not dissimilar in style from the Georgian one Kurt's family lived in, but Jambo and his mother had the bottom two floors only. Although the two floors were joined by a staircase, Jambo had his own entrance to the garden-floor flat, coming and going as he pleased, while his mother lived in the hall-floor flat. He was an only child and his parents had been divorced for years. His mother, Janice, was secretary and bookkeeper at the garden centre where Jambo worked and they saw one another every day at work.

This morning, realizing he was alone, Jambo dressed quickly and jumped from the bedroom window onto the garage roof. From there he leaped onto the back of the garden centre truck and landed agilely on the driveway. By the time Kurt returned with coffee and toast there was no sign of Jambo. Kurt took his coffee mug to the garage and surveyed what used to be his car. He picked up the boot lid, twisted and buckled from the petrol tank explosion. He had to earn some extra money to pay for repairs. It was about time he gigged again and he knew just which venue he would like to play first.

Natasha was also awake. She had a driving lesson booked with a new instructor Dawn's father had taken on. Natasha was used to her parents helping her out with most things but she knew they were deliberately dragging their feet over driving lessons. Neither of them wanted her to drive too soon, wishing to retain some control over her level of mobility and independence. Natasha had tried to argue that her mother, Jane, was married and having a baby at seventeen, the age Natasha was now, but Natasha's older sister, Rebecca, had tried this line of argument too many times and this merely led to the retort, 'Which is exactly how we know what goes on!' Natasha and Rebecca, who worked in London as a gopher for a radio station, had speculated that their parents, although idyllically happy together, had married in something of a rush, but neither parent would be drawn on the subject.

Tony, aiming to meet Julie before school, was another one awake unusually early, although Julie was already waiting at the kerbside outside her house,watching expectantly for him. Still a little unsure of himself, Tony wobbled his

Honda to a halt beside her. He did, however, manage to ride slowly along next to her on the way to school. When they arrived, Julie kissed him quickly before going into school. Tony was pleased but he could not help noticing that she had looked around first – to make sure no one saw? Supposing she was embarrassed to be seen with him? Lost in thought, Tony carried on to college, arriving at the same time as a Cunningham's Driving School car pulled smoothly up to the gates. Natasha got out and followed Tony into college. Catching up with him in the corridor she asked if he had happened to see Louise.

'Still wondering why the gods are picking on her?' Tony enquired. Natasha nodded. Tony thought about asking her advice – she did know Julie and she was pretty obviously female. Natasha realized he had something on his mind and waited expectantly but Tony thought better of mentioning it. 'It's nothing,' he smiled, seeing that she'd noticed his preoccupation. 'I better get on.'

Later that morning Natasha was still searching for Louise. Having exhausted every other possibility, she made for the toilets. Louise's usual cubicle was occupied. 'Here we go again,' she sighed, climbing onto the next door cistern.

'We can't go on meeting like this, Lou. What is it now?'

'Unless you've experienced pain, you can't possibly know,' came the sighing reply.

'What about witnessing the pain – for weeks? Does that count?'

Louise gave an even more long-suffering sigh but opened the door. She fished about in her bag and handed Natasha a piece of paper to read.

'You got a C in English?' Natasha finished reading.

'I always get As in English,' Louise cried.

In the canteen kitchen, Tony was trying to show Kurt the door.

'There's a new area manager around this week. You shouldn't be here. I'm not "mellowing" out for a year while my father supports me – so long as I'm still "planning" to go on to university.' Kurt acknowledged the dig. 'This is work. My future starts in there.'

'OK. I'm going,' Kurt said. 'I just came to see how you were getting on with Julie.'

Tony was suspicious. 'Is this more male bonding crap?'

'Curiosity. How is it going?'

'How are things going with you and Natasha?'

'As well as can be expected for two people who haven't spoken to each other.'

Tony was surprised. 'She couldn't have made it more obvious last week – with the Ragmoor Park tickets. Considering her usual response to you is "drop dead Benson" or "get lost Benson", I thought it showed progress.'

'True. It was just my natural modesty and sense of honour that prevented me from pointing out that she is desperate to get it together with me.'

'You don't want to appear too eager?'

'You have been listening and watching all these years then, Tone? It's all about respect – love, how you treat women.'

'Shall I get a notepad?'

But Kurt was starting to expound on his macho philosophy, 'I could just make a move on Natasha. But then what? She realizes she's a conquest and the whole self-esteem, feminist creed kicks in and it's over. Make them feel that you are the conquest and it's a different story. Let them buy the drinks, show a bit of vulnerability – all that new man stuff. Show you're in touch with your feminine side and with a small bit of luck, you could also be in touch with her feminine bits.'

'You've been reading too many women's magazines,' Tony had to smile. 'That and the fact you're scared of rejection.'

'Know thine enemy, Tone . . .' Kurt was interrupted by the other assistant chef. Tony was needed. 'I've got to see a guy about a gig, anyway.'

'What gig?'

'Guest spot, tonight. Be there! I'll let you know.'

Chapter 15

Natasha and Louise were sitting in the college canteen talking to two of their friends. Or rather Natasha was. Having finished her update on life without Joe, Louise was now avidly reading a horoscope hook. When the two girls left, Natasha interrupted Louise.

'Cheryl and Susie have gone . . . They said they'd love to stay and hear more about Joe but they wanted to go off,' Louise was not listening, '. . . have a career, get married, have kids.' Natasha grabbed the book and flung it away over her shoulder, 'Basically get a life!'

Louise at last looked up, shocked. Tony was also surprised, having been hit by the flying book. 'Sorry,' Natasha apologized.

Tony offered the book to Louise. 'What's up?' he asked.

'Have you ever been betrayed?' Louise marched out.

Natasha sighed, knowing she would have to go and nanny Louise once more. Before she went, Tony again started to ask her something. And again thought better of it. Natasha was intrigued. She was sure he wanted help with something. She liked Tony, he was level-headed and surprisingly sensitive – considering his choice of friends.

'I must go and check that Louise is all right. Make sure she isn't boring anyone else to death,' Natasha said. 'Look after my stuff. I'll be back.'

Tony smiled. Hopefully he would get the kind of advice he needed about Julie from someone who really knew.

Natasha hurried into the toilets. As she expected, Louise's cubicle was locked. Natasha went straight into the one next door, jumped onto the cistern and leaned over the partition. The cubicle was occupied – but not by Louise. Natasha and the girl who had seen her cajoling Louise several times before looked at one another, both equally shocked. Natasha almost fell down from the partition. She stumbled across to the door muttering 'Sorry!' and 'Big mistake' leaving before the girl, looking somewhat bewildered, appeared at the door.

Natasha, feeling acutely embarrassed, hurried back to the canteen to collect her bag and books keeping one eye on the door.

'O.K.?' Tony asked, wondering why Natasha looked so agitated. He was surprised when she jumped with fright. But she nodded in answer. Tony was concentrating on finding the right words to ask about Julie and did not notice Natasha's constant glances at the door. Her expression changed as the girl she had disturbed in the lavatory came into the canteen. Natasha turned and buried her head into Tony's chest.

'Hold me. Put your arms around me,' she hissed. Tony was somewhat taken aback but did as he was asked. Natasha muttered an explanation, but as most of it was directed at his armpit, Tony did not hear a word of it. Natasha also had her arms around Tony and when the girl passed by, she did not connect the embracing couple with the lunatic from the lavatory. She did not even think it odd that one half of the couple was one of the trainee chefs from the kitchen wearing a silly grin as he thought about the ridiculousness of the situation. It was just as well Kurt had paid his visit earlier. The other trainee chef who normally looked so disapproving if he caught Tony chatting or taking a break from work now watched him with a distinct expression of envy. Tony smiled and began to enjoy his protective role until Natasha pushed up his arm in order to peer out and survey the canteen.

'Has she gone?' she asked. Tony, who still did not know what she was talking about, looked blank. There was no sign of the girl and Natasha picked up the rest of her things.

'Thanks,' she said to Tony. 'But this never happened. O.K? Nothing.'

'Sure,' said Tony. 'Anytime. But what did happen?'

'Nothing!'

Tony handed Natasha Louise's astrology book. 'Who writes all that stuff?' he asked, realizing the moment to ask for advice had passed.

'It's not so much the people who write it we should worry about, it's the people who believe it,' Natasha went to the door, checked no one was about and left.

Tony was still confused. The other trainee chef was waiting for the tray of dirty dishes Tony had been collecting. Tony turned to him, 'Women,' he said. 'Don't make it too easy for them.' He took a plate from the tray, flicked it in the air, caught it and headed into the kitchen, leaving the trainee-chef admiring but slightly confused.

Dawn was just signing off a credit card receipt for her final customer of the day when Natasha arrived. Dawn began sorting papers, getting ready to lock up. Natasha flopped down into one of the sofas and sighed.

'I had a good driving lesson with the new bloke your dad's taken on – except he's got smelly breath,' Natasha pulled a face. 'Not that I'll be seeing that much of him, until I've saved up enough money for the next lesson.'

'You are getting a discount on account of you knowing the owner's daughter,' Dawn grinned. 'So what happened today?'

'Louise, basically,' Natasha sighed.

'She's still moping?' Dawn locked away the credit card vouchers.

'Hoping they'll make it an Olympic sport,' Natasha looked thoroughly fed up. 'I don't know what to do with her. I've tried everything I can think of and all I've achieved is that by now the whole college probably thinks I'm some kind of pervert,' Natasha grinned. 'I'll explain on the way. Are you coming out tonight?'

Dawn's face fell. She thought she ought to stay at home. She flipped off the lights and punched in the alarm code. Reluctantly she began to explain that she had been having trouble with Terry again.

Natasha was sympathetic. This was always a difficult subject. 'Why don't you just tell your mother?'

'Oh yeah. It's really simple. By the way Mum, your boyfriend is trying to grope me . . .' Natasha had heard it all before. 'Mum's spent too many years counselling other people to real- ize she needs it herself. She needs Terry, she wants to be appreciated, loved, understood. Anyway, I'm O.K. It's nothing I can't handle but I need to stay home for Cindy. Mum's out until late and Terry will be in this evening.'

'You could get Cindy to stay with one of her friends,' Natasha suggested.

'We'll see . . .' Dawn wanted to change the subject. She smiled brightly.

'Now – I can't imagine why everyone thinks you're a pervert. I'm all ears.'

Chapter 16

At nine o'clock that evening, Natasha's bedroom had its usual pre-evening out appearance.
Discarded clothes were scattered everywhere
and Natasha was in front of the mirror putting
the finishing touches to her make-up, Louise
was lounging on the bed, looking miserable and
still wearing the clothes she had worn to college.

There was a knock on the door and Dawn
came in, also dressed for an evening out.
Natasha was pleased to see her. 'There's been a
change of plan,' Dawn explained. 'Mum's meeting was cancelled and she and Terry are going
out. Cindy's got my number, so everything
should be fine.'

Dawn looked at Natasha and Louise and
neatly summed up the differences in their
appearances, 'What's this? Some kind of before
and after advert?'

'I didn't realize we were going out-out,'
Louise snapped, sulkily. 'I thought we were just
being out-in, downstairs.'

'Dad's got one of those pathetic bands he gets

on the cheap playing,' Natasha picked up some tickets. 'We're going to Studio Ten.'

In the bar, there were a few customers, including four young girls staring adoringly at the band.

'I see you haven't lost your touch as a rock promoter, Dad,' Natasha joked, grimacing about the music. 'What are you doing here?' she asked, as Tony walked over to the bar. It was only when Tony pointed to the band that Natasha realized it was Kurt singing and playing lead guitar. The session came to an end and Kurt joined the group at the bar.

'There's nothing like the sound of live music,' Greg said.

'And that was nothing like the sound of live music,' Natasha interrupted.

'Yeah. It was rubbish,' Kurt agreed.

'Did you write the last song yourself?' Dawn asked.

'As a matter of fact, yes,' said Kurt, perking up.

Dawn nodded. 'It was rubbish.'

Kurt spluttered into his drink, more through laughter than indignation. 'It was rubbish. But original rubbish. Where are you two going?' When he heard it was Studio Ten he shook his head. 'Bad music. Not rubbish but bad,' he turned to Louise. 'And where are you going?' This was more than Louise could take. She had looked bored at the banter anyway and now dived towards the lavatory.

Kurt was puzzled. 'What did I say?'

'She does that. A lot,' Tony commented.

'Your turn to go after her,' Natasha said to Dawn. 'I've been on "Lou" duty all day.'

Kurt still did not know what the problem was and Natasha began to explain. They sat in one of the window seats where they were soon interrupted by Jambo, taking his usual means of entry via a window. This time he ended up between Kurt and Natasha grinning at both of them.

'Do you have to do that?' Kurt asked. Jambo looked at the window, then he looked at Kurt and finally at Natasha. He realized Kurt was not talking about the window and slid out so that he was next to Tony and Kurt was once more next to Natasha.

'There must be something you can do to help Louise through this phase,' Kurt said.

'We are trying,' Natasha sighed.

'Who? What phase?' Jambo wanted to know what was going on.

'The trouble is, it's destiny,' Tony added in a mystic voice. 'It's in her stars.' Jambo began to look interested.

'Anything para-normal, supernatural, preordained . . . that's Louise,' said Natasha.

'She won't pull out of her depression until she "gets a sign",' Tony grinned.

'So why don't you use a ouija board?' asked Jambo, as if this was the most normal thing in the world to suggest. Everyone looked at him as though he were mad. 'You know . . . moving glass, knocks on table, funny voices, "one to one" with the spirit world. It sounds just the sort of thing for your friend.'

'You've got a direct line to the dead have you?' said Natasha sarcastically.

'Dead cert,' said Jambo.

'Dead stupid,' Natasha dismissed him.

Kurt and Tony laughed. But Jambo was serious and had an idea about how to make the glass move. Kurt had a remote control gadget which was a motor and radio receiver strapped together above a set of wheels. It was very small and if they were careful about what glass they chose, it would not be seen. All they had to do was to work out how to control it. They all began to see that Jambo's mad suggestion might just work. The next question was where to hold the seance.

'Why not . . . right here?' Kurt spoke in a mock spooky tone.

'I'm sure I can persuade my dad,' Natasha wiggled her little finger.

Kurt went home to fetch the remote-control car while Jambo worked out how to log-on to the spirit net without detection.

'You find a way to keep Louise here, subtly,' Kurt instructed Tony.

Tony grinned. From what he knew of Louise there was no need to be subtle. 'Hey Louise,' he called as she came back into the bar. 'Fancy having a go on a ouija board?'

For the first time in weeks, Louise looked enthusiastic. Kurt looked impressed.

Later, at closing time, Greg was collecting glasses and ushering out the last of the customers. Out of sight of Louise, Jambo was fiddling with cables and putting the finishing touches to the spirit network. Dawn, who had been filled in on the plan, and Louise were cutting out letters for the board.

Natasha was at the bar pouring drinks with Tony. 'Where's Julie tonight?' she asked.

'Textiles project.'

'So's Sarah,' Natasha said. 'Sorry about earlier today. Did you want to talk about anything in particular?'

Tony looked a little embarrassed. He pointed upstairs. 'Well, not your sister . . . her mate.'

Natasha tried not to smile. 'What about her mate?'

Tony again looked embarrassed. He did not know how to begin. 'I'm just not sure . . . It's something to do with being around God's gift to women all the time . . .'

Natasha nodded encouragingly. 'In Kurt's own opinion I presume.'

Tony grinned. 'Legend in his own lunchtime. But . . . he is confident. You can't deny that. And I'm not. Kurt really knows it all, you know – what makes women tick,' Natasha was now really intrigued and smiled understandingly. 'Stuff like "knowing your enemy", like letting women do all the chasing so they won't feel like a conquest when he . . . well you know.'

'Yes. I think I do,' Natasha's smile had a fixed quality about it and her tone was clipped. Tony bit his lip, worried he had said too much. To reassure him, Natasha turned the conversation back to him, 'But you don't feel that attitude is right for you and Julie? Do you want some advice from "one of the enemy"? Just be yourself. You're really nice.' She smiled and kissed his cheek, just as Kurt arrived back.

'I don't want to be "nice". I want to be sexy,' Tony protested.

'What's going on here, Hutchinson?' Kurt was curious and just a little jealous.

'If you will leave me alone with these women,' Tony grinned smugly. It was not often that Kurt was envious of him.

Kurt was puzzled but went to find Jambo to put the finishing touches to the arrangements. Natasha was reassuring her father, who was having second thoughts about letting them carry on.

It's only a bit of harmless fun. It's all about the power of auto-suggestion and the susceptibility of the participating parties,' she said, hugging him. 'And with a bit of luck, it will be just what Louise needs to cheer her up.'

Tony found Kurt in the pub corridor demonstrating to Jambo how to move a large frosted lager glass with the remote control. 'We'll keep our fingers on top of the glass and slow it down a bit. Make quick jabs with the control. That should keep the noise down.'

'How did you get it to work?' Tony asked.

Kurt showed him how he had taken out the motor and receiver and strapped them together. He had used a piece of tissue paper to deaden the noise of the motor.

'We're ready. Let's go,' Kurt said. He handed the control to Jambo, picked up the motorized glass and went into the bar with Tony, turning back at the door to take the microphone from Jambo who liked the idea of spooky, supernatural sound effects. Kurt could just imagine how subtle they would be and could see Jambo blowing the whole thing.

The lights were dimmed, and the paper letters were arranged in a circle on a round table. Everyone had carefully positioned themselves with Kurt between Louise and Natasha, and Dawn opposite. This meant they could all make eye contact and watch for Louise's reaction. The glass began to move erratically. Jambo had not quite got the hang of the controls and was having difficulty seeing the table from the corridor through the gloom.

'Who's doing that?' Louise jumped.

'No one . . . in this room,' Kurt answered truthfully. He could not resist adding, 'It's a pity Jambo couldn't stay. He loves all this weird stuff – X-*Files, Outer Limits . . . Zig and Zag.'*

The others all looked at him. What was he on about? Kurt shrugged. Everyone had taken their hands off the glass. Suddenly it began to move.

'It moved by itself!' Louise shrieked.

'Not by itself Louise . . . with help,' Kurt looked up, theatrically. He was beginning to enjoy himself.

Natasha, who had been watching Louise, was beginning to feel uneasy. Louise was starting to believe something was happening. She was concerned that what had started as a harmless joke was going to develop into something hurtful. Louise was hooked.

'Do you think so?' she said breathlessly to Kurt. 'Do you think it could help me?'

'Definitely,' said Kurt, in full flow now and feeling confident. 'We'll give it one more try. Let's ask it a simple question like: Is Joe the only guy you're ever destined to go out with? And, if not, then will you meet someone else soon,' Kurt paused and thought again, 'Well if not soon, then eventually,' he thought again. 'In the not too distant future?'

'Sounds a simple question,' said Tony.

Kurt continued, 'If we are still in connection with the spirit . . . Hey! Spirit Dude.'

Natasha nudged him. He was going too far. They all settled down again and waited . . . and waited. Nothing happened.

'Hello,' Louise said tentatively. Then in answer to the others' dubious looks, 'Well what else would you say?'

'Perhaps we could call up spirit enquiries –

"Which spirit please?", "The spirit you require is . . .",' Tony joked.

But even he jumped when Jambo moved the glass again.

'Let's see if we summon up a Red Indian or a Saxon Warrior . . .' Kurt said.

This began a lengthy debate about whether spirits only came from the past and whether they could come from the future. Louise was impatient to get on and ask questions about her own future. 'Spirits can't come from the future because the future doesn't exist yet,' she sounded irritated.

'But in the space-time continuum the future does exist and spirits must be able to time travel,' Tony was interested in the debate and beginning to forget why they were all there.

Even Dawn was curious. 'Why?' she asked.

'Because if we do get a Red Indian . . .' Tony explained.

'Or a Saxon Warrior,' Kurt added flippantly.

'Then they would have travelled forward to the future, wouldn't they?' Tony concluded.

Louise was even more irritated and impatient but she could not ignore the argument. 'That's because it's our past, it exists. Now can we get on?' Tony was about to say something else when Louise silenced him, 'If you don't shut up you'll experience the space-time continuum first hand in a minute. What shall we ask?'

'Well I think it's worth asking about this future business . . .' Tony began. Everyone glared at him. Kurt, who was opposite, shook his head and mouthed 'It isn't real, remember?' Tony looked shame-faced as he clicked out of it.

Jambo meanwhile was getting cold in the corridor and was bored with waiting. He decided to move the glass anyway. He still could not see all the letters very well and spelt out L-O-O.

'It wants the loo?! Tony tried not to laugh.

'Lou – Louise, idiot,' Dawn hissed at him.

'Oh! That's me!' cried Louise. Dawn pulled a 'pitiful' face and Natasha began to feel very uneasy.

'Hello . . .' Louise couldn't think how to address the spirit.

'Try "Running Buffalo",' Tony sniggered. Kurt threw a beer mat across at him and a warning look.

If Louise had turned around at this point, she would have seen Jambo leaning forward from the shadows straining to see the table. The glass moved to X and then twisted around before going to Y. This was not what Jambo had in mind. Kurt thought quickly.

'Y for yes!' he explained. The glass twitched. Everyone looked expectant . . . so what?

Kurt thought again. 'It means – Yes, it can tell her a lot?' The glass twitched again seeming to imply that Kurt was right.

'Can you tell me if I will ever be happy again?' Louise was enthralled.

Jambo moved the glass back and forward against the Y. Louise was really excited and had almost forgotten the others were there. Kurt and Tony grinned, delighted the scam was working so well. But Dawn was beginning to feel uncomfortable and Natasha felt the whole thing had gone far enough.

'I think we should stop now,' she said.

'Why?' asked Kurt and Tony together. 'It's working brilliantly. It's only a bit of fun.'

'It's not right,' said Dawn.

Although it should have been obvious what they were talking about, Louise was far too wrapped up in it all to notice.

'Will I ever love again?' she asked.

Jambo moved the glass back and forward against the Y again. Louise was delighted. Natasha and Dawn were concerned. 'What shall I ask next?' asked Louise.

Natasha made a decision. She wanted to finish the seance. 'I know. One last but crucial question – what is the name of Louise's next boyfriend?'

Kurt was happy to go along with this but Tony sensed Natasha was up to something. He shifted uneasily suspecting that it might be a result of his earlier conversation with her. He knew he had said too much. Trying to give a warning he objected, 'But that would mean the spirit would have to go into the future.'

Natasha, however, was determined. She silenced him with a look and then realizing that Louise also wanted an answer, she explained. 'It doesn't have to travel, it can just peep into the future, like a live satellite link.'

Kurt and Dawn pulled faces. Louise would never fall for such a weak line. But Louise seemed quite happy. This obviously passed the space-time continuum test, especially as she wanted to know the answer.

'Who will I go out with next?' Louise spoke intently to the glass.

Before the glass moved, Natasha put both hands on it as if to stop it. She looked around the table at Tony, Dawn, Louise and Kurt in turn. 'Before we get the answer, we must agree: this is the last question and we all accept the advice of the spirit.'

Tony looked worried, Dawn shrugged, Louise nodded earnestly and Kurt felt uneasy. A faint warning, a suspicion of a trap. He hesitated and then glanced at Natasha. She smiled and looked intently at him. He saw his face mirrored in her large grey eyes. He would have agreed to anything. And said coolly, 'Hey . . . we are only here to help.'

'In any way we can, right?' Natasha spoke softly. 'O.K. Louise. Ask away.'

Louise seemed to summon all her strength. She was breathless with excitement as she repeated her question. For a moment the glass did not move as Jambo was not at all sure what to do. Slowly it began to move around the table. Both Dawn and Natasha quickly realized Kurt was moving it. Even Louise was suspicious.

'Are you moving it?' she asked.

'Absolutely not. Look,' he spoke louder so that Jambo would get the message and took his hand from the glass. 'It's moving of its own accord.' Sure enough, the glass was moving, now under Jambo's control.

'Your fate lies in that glass,' Kurt was enjoying himself again.

'And we are all bound by its outcome?' Natasha asked.

'Absolutely. This is the perfect situation. Your future fate and happiness are about to be decided,' Kurt, the condemned man, spoke obliviously, sealing his fate.

Natasha looked significantly at Dawn then flicked her eyes towards Kurt. Dawn immediately picked up what Natasha meant and the two of them begin to guide the glass.

'It's going to a K,' said Kurt happily, not suspecting a thing. 'Now a U . . .' It was then he realized what was going on. He dived forward to put his hand on the glass, but too late.

'R,' said Louise. She did not need any more letters. She stopped, stared at Kurt and jumped on him. Kurt was knocked backwards as Louise sat on his lap.

'No, no Louise, I think there's been a mistake,' Louise was not listening.

Natasha leaned across to Dawn and smiled, 'Know your enemy!!'

Chapter 17

On Saturday morning Jambo was out making a
delivery. Driving down a country road, in his
green garden centre truck with plants loaded
onto the back he hummed along to his walkman
while the countryside passed as if he had not a
care in the world. He liked being in the open air,
on his own with no one breathing down his
neck, telling him what to do. He was passing a
field of grazing cows when something caught
his eye. He slammed on the brakes and
screeched to a halt. He took another look and a
wicked grin spread across his face. The question
was, could he get it into the back of the truck?
There was no one around and ten minutes later
Jambo set off once more, very pleased with himself and his find.

For once, Dawn had a free Saturday when she
was not expected at work. Her morning, however, had not got off to a good start. There had
been a scene with Terry again. Her mother had
discovered them arguing and sided with Terry.
Dawn was furious. She let herself out of the

back door, slamming it behind her, pulling on her jacket as she went. She hurried around the side of the house and ran straight into her mother who had come out of the front door to intercept her. Angela grabbed her arm and mother and daughter stood face to face glaring at one another. Apart from the fact that they were both equally strong-minded and determined, they were not very alike. They certainly did not look alike – Angela's red curls were a bright contrast to Dawn's short, almost black bob. Green eyes confronted brown. In character Dawn was pragmatic and practical and her mother was increasingly emotional and irrational. Both waited for the other to speak first but before either said a word, Terry appeared in the doorway. He slouched against the door frame regarding Dawn with a mocking grin. The grin switched instantly to a look of concern when Angela turned round. Both women sensed the moment for talking had passed. Dawn hurried away leaving her mother to be comforted by Terry.

At the bus stop Dawn pulled out her mobile phone and dialled Natasha's number. The phone rang for ages before a sleepy voice answered. Dawn was relieved.

'I thought you weren't there,' now that she was no longer angry, she felt like crying. 'I wondered if you could meet me . . . I can't explain now.' There were two other women standing nearby also waiting for a bus. They were obviously curious but trying not to appear to be listening. From their sympathetic expressions they probably thought she was talking to a boyfriend. Dawn smiled politely in response but sat well away from them when the bus arrived.

Half an hour later Natasha was dressed and made up, and hurrying along Souter Street, past the river cruisers, making for the cafe next to the river where she had arranged to meet Dawn.

'What's up?' she asked when she found Dawn. After a brisk walk by the river to the cafe Dawn was feeling much better. 'I'm O.K. now,' she said.

'So why did you get me up early?' Natasha tried to encourage Dawn to talk.

'That's the difference between work and college – when I have a day off I want to enjoy every moment. Even if it means getting up early,' Dawn said, avoiding the subject.

'It didn't sound like you were enjoying much this morning,' Natasha knew her friend too well to be fooled. 'Come on. I'll buy you a coffee. Tell me all about it. I assume it's about your mum's "toyboy". Well ... I didn't give up my warm bed to dash down here and be told its's "O.K. now". You work out what to tell me while I get the drinks, even if you have to make it up to keep me quiet,' this at least made Dawn smile.

Natasha went off to buy two large, frothy cappuccinos with lots of chocolate on top while Dawn found a table. She chose one that was well away from anyone else and sat down with a sigh, facing the river. She watched a family of ducks paddle along the bank occasionally diving for food, wishing her own life was as carefree and simple.

Kurt was at home having a late breakfast. He was lounging in the kitchen, sitting with his feet up at the table munching his way through his third bowl of Sugar Puffs. The TV was blasting away on one worktop and the radio blaring equally loudly from another. Kurt was also reading *Melody Maker*, drinking his second mug of coffee and talking on the phone.

'I'll let you know . . . in about five minutes,' Kurt spoke into the handset as his mother walked in. She grimaced at the level of noise, picked up the remote control from the table next to Kurt's cereal bowl and switched off the TV. She flipped the sound down on the radio and turned to Kurt.

'I don't understand how you can watch TV and listen to the radio while reading and talking on the telephone!' She sounded exasperated and flicked at his feet still resting on the chair. 'Your father isn't subsidising your year off so that you can squander it sitting around wasting electricity and running up phone bills.'

Kurt sighed. He had heard it all before. He dropped his feet down from the chair, reached for the remote control and put the television back on but at a lower volume. He then concluded his telephone conversation.

'It's one of those creatures that devours its young,' he grinned at his mother. 'I'll call you back.'

Juliet Benson glared at Kurt. She was sharp-featured as well as sharp-tongued and well used to dealing with her eldest son, and his sister and brother who she now called down from their rooms. She was attractive and looked younger than her forty-two years. Today, she was smartly dressed and from the large leather holdall in the hallway, it was obvious she was going away. Juliet turned back to Kurt who was preparing himself for one of his 'clever' conversations with his mother.

'I was filling the gaps between concentration spans,' he said, pouring milk into yet another bowl of cereal.

'You're wasting milk. You're supposed to have one bowl of cereal,' Juliet checked her watch, 'and for breakfast, not lunch.'

'Traditionalist convention,' Kurt spoke dismissively. 'The only thing I'm wasting by going to and from the fridge is intellectual capacity. Walking is a motor-reflex. I do not need to think about it, so while suspending my intellectual concentration on the music press I can take in the audio and visual stimuli from the radio and television.'

'You mean they were on when you came in and you couldn't be bothered to turn them off,' she said sarcastically. Kurt nodded his agreement that this might just be a valid hypothesis.

'Did you get the message that Louise called?'

Kurt groaned, 'Top of the hour every hour.'

'She sounded like a nice girl,' Juliet was fishing for information. Largely due to the fact that Kurt's girlfriends changed with incredible frequency, she rarely got to know very much about them. Things had also been abnormally quiet recently. Kurt did not appear to be seeing anyone and Juliet had suspected there was someone he was more than usually serious about. Certainly, Louise had sounded rather different from Kurt's other girlfriends. Kurt grimaced. Louise was just the sort of girl his mother would like.

'Just don't ask, Mother,' he snapped.

Juliet was just about to call Lucy and Ollie again when Lucy bounced into the kitchen.

'Did Mum tell you Louise called again, Kurt?' she grinned mischievously. Kurt glared.

'Where's Oliver?' Juliet asked.

'Probably in the bathroom with my magazines, as usual,' Lucy shrugged.

Kurt sniggered until his mother gave him a withering look. Lucy flicked through the channels to protests from Kurt that he was watching. It was now his mother's turn to laugh as Lucy said, 'You can't possibly do three things at once.'

'It's probably a male thing,' Kurt began as both women looked scathingly at him. He was interrupted by Ollie who slouched in, wearing his out-of-school clothes and favourite cap.

'How's your eyesight, Ol?' Kurt smirked. Ollie pulled a 'very funny' type face and asked if Kurt knew that Louise had called – five times. Kurt threw a magazine at him. Like Lucy, Ollie was delighted to have something to tease Kurt about.

'What time did your father say he'd be finished?' Juliet asked her daughter. Lucy worked with her father, Kirk, in his wholesale electrical business.

'He's checking the multi-media PCs that just came in but he should be finished about one,' she replied.

It was almost time for Juliet to leave. She and Kirk were going away for the weekend to a country house hotel in the Lake District.

'Right, while you are all in the same room,' Juliet silenced the TV, switched off the radio and gestured to Ollie to pick up the magazine he had just lobbed back at Kurt. 'Can I have your undivided attention for one moment. Your father and I are looking forward to this weekend away. We don't want it spoiled by coming back to find the house looking like a tip! Clear?'

She looked at each of them in turn. They nodded. She went to kiss each of them in turn. She received a hug from Lucy, tolerance from Ollie and then hesitated at Kurt. He showed no sign of moving towards her and she thought better of it. She looked at them all again, feeling rather suspicious, wondering if she was having a premonition but they looked the picture of innocence. With a deep breath she made up her mind to go and was pleasantly surprised by Kurt who stood up and asked if she wanted help with her bag.

'Oliver! Your mother's bag, and quick about it!' he ordered.

'You're so considerate,' Juliet said sarcastically.

'You did a great job raising me, Ma,' Kurt grinned back and hugged her. Juliet still looked concerned.

'Mother,' Lucy spoke reassuringly. 'I'll be here.' Kurt groaned at her but this seemed to do the trick. Juliet left and at the sound of the car tyres moving on the gravel drive, Kurt picked up the phone and pressed redial.

'Is it on?' Lucy asked.

'As long as your lot bring their own drink.'

Smiling, Lucy spun round and dashed out – to spread the word.

'Toe-nee!' Kurt resumed his earlier conversation. 'It's on. Nine o'clock till late! Rave to the grave!'

Ollie had passed Lucy on her way out and now overheard Kurt on the phone. He guessed correctly what was being planned.

'What about me?' he asked hopefully.

'What about you?'

'I'll only bring a few . . .'

'Too young. You are going to be out!' With that Kurt headed for the door. The grin on Ollie's face when Kurt had gone made it clear that he had not the slightest intention of taking 'no' for an answer.

Later that morning Kurt was busily emptying the fridge of all non-perishable items as instructed by Tony who was bringing food for the party. He was also continuing to demonstrate his ability to do more than one thing at the same time. The radio was playing loudly and he was again talking on the phone. Inviting yet more people.

'It's not a party – it's a gathering. Just you and a partner. See you later,' Kurt explained and hung up. The phone immediately began to ring.

Lucy was about to go out into Chester, shopping. While Kurt was preoccupied she decided it would be the ideal moment to ask about the evening. She chose her words carefully.

'So you don't mind if I bring twelve tonight then?' she concluded.

'. . . Just you and your partner,' Kurt finished his spiel and, realizing what Lucy had said, hurried after her. 'How many?' he asked, catching up with her in the hall. The phone which Kurt was still holding began to ring again. 'I'm listening,' he spoke to the phone and then turned to Lucy, 'What genders?'

'Nine female,' Lucy grinned. 'I'm not sure about the other three.'

Kurt nodded his agreement and turned his full attention back to the phone, 'Yeah, I heard,' he said.

'And you heard him in case he changes his mind or gets stressed later,' Lucy smiled at Tony, 'And don't mention Louise to him.'

Tony was dressed for work in his trainee chef's uniform. He was depositing a large cardboard box of food in the hallway next to a stack of others which he had just brought in along with various items of catering equipment.

'Who was that on the phone?' Tony asked Kurt.

'Jambo. He wanted to know if he could bring a "friend" – some "right cow" he'd just met. Sounds great!' Kurt was looking at the boxes of food in amazement. 'I said a few nibbles, Tone, not a UN relief convoy.'

'If you want me to cater, I cater,' Tony began shifting the boxes through to the kitchen. Kurt was puzzled as to how Tony had got everything to the house. It certainly wouldn't have fitted on his Honda. But the phone was begging to be answered again.

'. . . Just you and a partner,' Kurt said for the umpteenth time that morning. He hung up.

'Is she coming?' Tony asked tentatively. He referred to Louise. Kurt gave him a warning look. This was not his favourite topic of conversation. 'You renewed her faith in life, remember?'

'I did it to hand her back her dignity. It's called empowerment. I wanted her to get a life – but it wasn't supposed to be mine,' Kurt answered the phone. 'Yep, yep, that's right. It's a gathering. Just you and a partner.'

Kurt lifted a corner of the tissue covering the tray Tony was carrying. He peered underneath and saw rows of perfectly made choux pastry swans filled with cream and fruit. Tony had gone to a great deal of trouble over the food for this evening and Kurt was not at all sure that it was all for his benefit. He rather suspected that Tony wanted to impress someone else. Kurt smirked. You did not need to be a genius to work out who.

Tony was still joking about Kurt and Louise. 'You can't go against fate. You two were brought together by the heavenly spirits,' he laughed.

'I was stitched up by earthly bodies!' Kurt protested.

'You agreed to help Natasha sort out Louise.'

'With the aim of ending up with Natasha.' He lifted a bottle from one of the boxes and counted the bottles. 'Cutting back are you? Best behaviour time?' he quizzed.

'Julie will be here,' Tony said, a little defensively. 'What about Ollie?'

'He's never on his best behaviour,' Kurt grinned. 'Relax, Tone. He's been exiled for the night. Anyway Julie's your girlfriend now,' Kurt answered the phone. 'How did you find out?' Kurt grinned and proceeded to argue a deal with the person on the other end of the line. 'O.K. But sorted music and none of that bogus Jungle rubbish . . . Guitars, man. They're the whole basis of modern music . . . Here's the deal. No live transmision from the house . . . Because I live here with my mother . . . No more than ten minutes in every hour then and each set separated by fifty minutes. So don't try backing ten minutes from one hour against ten from the next . . . Been around you too long, Bazz,' Kurt grinned, flicked the 'off' switch and slammed down the aerial. Kurt grinned at Tony. 'Food, drink, music – done. Now, how did Bazz find out about tonight? And just how did you get everything round here?'

Tony grinned and beckoned Kurt to the door. There, in front of the house was the purple Bazz FM road show vehicle. Bazz was sitting on the tailboard nonchalantly swinging his legs. He grinned and waved his phone. Kurt laughed, enjoying the set up. Kurt was looking forward to this evening. The one black spot being Louise. Somehow he had to convince her that she no longer wanted to go out with him without hurting her feelings or plunging her back into the depths of despair.

Chapter 18

Two hours, two cappuccinos and a croissant each later and Dawn and Natasha were still discussing Terry.

'It was just like the time he walked in on me in the bathroom,' Dawn shuddered at the memory. 'He always makes out that it's some misunderstanding, that he's embarrassed. If it is, it takes at least five minutes for him to blush. It's his creepy manner,' Dawn trailed off.

'But he's never actually done anything?' Natasha was sympathetic but there seemed nothing concrete to accuse Terry of.

'He brushes up against us, he walks into rooms unannounced, he tries to get either Cindy or me on our own. It's all part of the same thing,' Dawn sighed. 'Cindy thinks the same but at fourteen she doesn't really believe it's happening. Maybe I over-react because he makes my skin crawl. But you've seen the sleazy way he looks at you. Anyway, I get the call about Kurt's party so I tell Mum I'll be out tonight. Cindy will be babysitting Max because Mum and the jerk are also going out. The next thing is the jerk says he'll pop back during the evening to make sure Cindy and Max are O.K.' Natasha just looked at her friend trying to make some sense of it all. 'I know,' Dawn continued. 'It makes me sound paranoid. But I just don't trust him in the house alone with Cindy.'

'If you can't talk to your mum, what about your dad?'

'He'd go ballistic. We'd all end up in court again and meanwhile, we've all got to live with Mum and the jerk. Besides, Dad's away for a week.'

'What are you going to do then?'

'Same as usual. Nothing. Stay home. Make sure Cindy's O.K. and miss the party tonight,' Dawn ended miserably.

The two girls drained the last of their coffees and walked into Chester. They strolled slowly along the half-timbered lanes, too busy talking to notice the shop windows they were passing.

'You can't keep staying in. You might be over-reacting. You could bring Cindy with you. Benson won't mind – she is female,' Natasha said. Before Dawn could reply, they were interrupted by Maddie.

'I thought you were covering for me in the shop today?' Dawn sounded cross and accusing.

'Mum's there and it's the lunch hour. What's wrong with you today?' Maddie was surprised at Dawn. 'Are you two going to Benson's bash tonight?'

'How did you know about it?' asked Natasha, curiously.

'I am on the net. I suppose Louise will be there,' Maddie looked at Natasha teasingly. 'Now that she's "going steady" with Kurt.'

'I don't think they're "going steady",' Natasha felt needled. She did not know why she should mind – it was all because of her joke after all. And it was not as if she and Kurt were an item.

Dawn registered Natasha's reaction and realized Natasha was not nearly as cool about Benson as she liked to think.

Maddie was obviously enjoying herself. 'I thought it was pre-ordained destiny, that the spirit world decreed it – a match made in the celestial heavens. According to Louise that is. Anyway, I must dash. I've only got an hour to find a new hunting outfit for tonight.'

Back at Benson's, preparations for the 'gathering' were well under way. Bazz was starting to bring in the equipment for the Bazz FM sound and light show. Kurt was finishing yet another telephone call. 'I'm starving,' he said. 'Can I just try one of those swan things.'

'No,' said Tony. 'They're for tonight and make sure they stay in the fridge. And get down from there, you'll damage the brie.'

'I must say Anthony, old chap, you'll make somebody a wonderful wife. Does Julie know you're like this?' Kurt's attention was then caught by Bazz dropping several coils of cable on the floor. 'I hope those are clean. I don't want any grubby marks anywhere.'

'Does Louise know you're like that?!' Tony laughed and Kurt just gritted his teeth. The expression froze on his face as Louise appeared at the door. She held out a bunch of flowers for the party. Kurt looked acutely embarrassed. Tony tried not to snigger.

'Did you miss me?' Louise asked, hugging Kurt and resting her head against his chest.

'I couldn't find the words to describe it,' Kurt spoke over her head at the now openly sniggering Tony. Louise squeezed tighter.

When he had eventually managed to disentangle himself, Kurt went to find Tony, who'd retired to the kitchen. The situation with Louise required drastic action and the sooner the better. Kurt was not sure how much more he could put up with. The trouble was every time he went to say something she looked up at him with her trusting soft brown eyes and he just could not bring himself to do anything that would make them fill with tears. Tony smiled. He had known Kurt a long time and knew very well that, under that macho cool exterior, Kurt was surprisingly sensitive, and much more considerate than most people suspected.

'So where is Louise?' he asked.

'Gone to buy a new dress, so I'll be proud of her,' Kurt sighed. 'It's unbelievable.'

'You're going to have to get out of that soon,'

Tony said, sympathetically. Kurt just nodded. 'Don't I know it.'

Ollie arrived back from his usual Saturday habit of hanging around with his mates. He glowered at his enemy, Tony.

'It's time to start growing up, Ollie. You've been binned by Julie for Tony. That's life. It's not fair, it sucks but that's it,' Kurt was not going to let Ollie start causing trouble.

Tony felt embarrassed and guilty about the whole affair. Julie had already finished with Ollie when he asked her out but he hadn't known that when he first spoke to her. He guessed Ollie must be feeling pretty miserable.

'I'm sorry,' Tony said.

'She was fine until you came along,' Ollie was bitter.

'She was fine until you tried to kill her in my car, remember?' Kurt corrected Ollie. 'And she's coming tonight which is why you aren't. Now, disappear!'

There was a particularly loud thud and Bazz appeared with a speaker attached to a cable. Ollie took advantage of the diversion to slink away. Bazz was completely immersed in what he was doing and oblivious to any atmosphere, just as he had not noticed any awkwardness over Louise. Now he put down the speaker and surveyed the room to decide where the best position for his speaker would be. He finally settled on a spot on the wall next to the door frame. He was just about to start hammering in a bracket when Kurt realized what he was doing.

'Freeze!' Kurt yelled. 'I said no marks. Have you met my mother? Do you want to get me killed?'

'This isn't a good idea, right?' Bazz asked, coolly. 'How am I going to get sound into the kitchen?'

Kurt suggested the floor. Bazz was about to protest, when he saw Kurt's expression. He decided not to push the issue. 'On the floor is good,' he said.

Kurt meanwhile began to wonder what else Bazz had rigged up. He went into the hall to investigate. Wires and cables were everywhere, they ran up and down the stairs, into every room and were draped over the banisters. In addition the mixing desk, which was propped on various custom-made boxes, completely blocked the stairs. The technological spider's web spread out in front of Kurt was truly incredible. The sound from it might well be amazing. But . . . there was absolutely no room for any guests. Seeing the problem, Bazz began to rearrange his equipment.

Chapter 19

By nine-thirty that evening, the Benson house was throbbing. Kurt might have called it a gathering but it looked like Glastonbury. The chances of one of the neighbours not reporting the noise and numbers of people to Mr and Mrs Benson were pretty slim. Kurt was standing at the foot of the stairs where he could watch most rooms. The Bazz FM sound desk was now in the living room and Bazz was just drawing to the end of one of his ten-minute slots. Kurt glanced across at him and tapped his watch. Bazz grinned and pumped up the volume. Kurt glared. Bazz grinned even more broadly and took the microphone.

'Ree-al mue-zak . . . Rhythm of the civilized world,' he whooped. Then added looking at Kurt, 'Now for the less adventurous, let's choke on a bit of the heavenly knight, Sir . . . Clifford of Richard.'

Kurt pulled a face as the jungle-rap faded, to be replaced by – Oasis thrash guitars. Bazz grinned again and mouthed 'Gotcha!' at Kurt. All seemed to be going well, Kurt began to relax, and then Louise arrived. Her curly brown hair was caught up on top of her head, she was wearing a pink floral dress. She looked pretty, a 'nice' girl, like every mother's dream – but not like Kurt's. His heart sank. He cringed as, smiling, Louise pushed her way through the crowd towards him.

Natasha was at Dawn's house dressed to party. Her gleaming blonde hair was clipped back to one side and she was wearing a strappy black top and trousers with a green jacket. She was trying to persuade Dawn to come along when Terry walked in, also dressed to go out. He cast a long appreciative look at Natasha before he winked and turned to Dawn to tell her there was someone else to see her.

'Yeuch!' Natasha pulled a face at Dawn. Maddie swished into the room looking amazing. Terry couldn't keep his eyes off her and was practically drooling. 'Going somewhere special?' he asked. Maddie smiled briefly. 'Pity I can't come,' Terry added.

Maddie looked dismissively at him. 'A few more minutes and you probably will,' she said, coldly.

Natasha had to look away to hide her smile. Trust Maddie!

'You can go, too, Dawn. I said I'd pop back to check on Cindy and Max,' Terry said, unfazed by Maddie's reaction.

'No. It's fine. I don't want to,' Dawn said.

With a last, lingering look at Maddie, Terry left.

'What a creep!' Maddie said. 'What does your mother see in him? He really fancies himself.'

'If only that was all he fancied,' Dawn looked thoroughly depressed.

'Aren't you coming?' Maddie asked, puzzled. It was not like Dawn to choose to stay in. 'A good night out will cheer you up.'

Dawn shook her head and Natasha immediately said she would stay too.

'What about leaving Benson alone with Louise?' asked Dawn with a knowing grin.

'She's gone mental over him hasn't she?' Maddie exclaimed. 'What happened with that ouija board session?'

'It was a stupid idea. You know how obsessed she is with anything to do with horoscopes and the supernatural,' Natasha sounded as if she regretted the whole episode. 'We just thought it might help her get over that idiot, Joe. It started as a joke.'

'And you wanted to sort out Benson,' Dawn pointed out. 'I'm surprised he's put up with it for a whole week.'

'He's not as tough as he likes to think he is,' Natasha smiled. She was the second person that day to reach that conclusion about Kurt. 'He's probably frightened that she will kill herself if he rejects her as well.'

'You wicked bitch. You'll have to go along, if only to see how he's coping,' Maddie laughed.

It was obvious that Natasha wanted to go and it was only concern for Dawn that was stopping her. She suggested that they could go along after Dawn's mum came home. Maddie looked at them both suspiciously.

'What's going on?' she asked, putting the kettle on. 'Something is. And I'm not going now until I find out.'

By the time Maddie had finished her coffee, Dawn had finished giving her the background on Terry. 'He's always been the same,' Dawn concluded. 'But he's been a lot worse over the last year.'

'I could see he had that look about him,' Maddie was thoughtful. 'There's only one answer – we'll take the kids with us.'

Natasha and Dawn looked startled and unconvinced.

'Benson would go ape,' Natasha mimicked him. '"Just you and a partner".'

Maddie didn't see the problem. Dawn could take Cindy and she would take Max, 'Leaving you free to concentrate on Benson, Natasha!'

Natasha almost blushed and began to stammer a denial of any interest in Kurt, not convincing anyone. Dawn objected because Cindy and Max were too young. But Maddie had thought of everything. She even offered to run them home early as soon as Dawn's mother was back. Natasha looked hopeful, Dawn was still undecided.

'Go!' Maddie ordered. 'Get ready. It'll be fine!' Dawn went.

At the party, Kurt was busy being busy, trying to avoid Louise. Tony, no longer wearing his chef's uniform, was trying to make his way across the kitchen to Julie, carrying a tray of swans. As he picked his way between revellers, hands reached out to grab swans. When he reached Julie, there was only one left.

'Tony, it's lovely,' Julie seemed impressed.

'I made them for you,' Tony said modestly.

Julie stared at Tony. Tony stared at Julie. They leaned towards one another, when suddenly, 'Can I have that duck, mate?' the moment was spoiled. Tony swung the tray out of reach and towards Julie. 'You'd better take it before . . .'

Someone else grabbed the swan and disappeared into the throng. Tony swirled around but Julie pulled him back. 'It doesn't matter,' she whispered. 'Come here.' She kissed him gently. Tony forgot all about swans and food, put his arms around her and pulled her close. 'You're lovely,' he murmured.

They were soon disturbed, this time by a loud cheer from the hall. Tony and Julie followed the crowd rushing out to see what was going on. They soon spotted the cause of the hilarity. First the head and then the entire body of a large black and white model cow appeared through the front door and then proceeded along the hall. It seemed to be moving on its own until Jambo's head popped up from behind its tail, grinning.

'Bolton!' Kurt yelled.

'You said I could bring a partner. This is Margaret!' Jambo grinned, pleased at the response his joke was getting.

Kurt laughed, '"The right cow'!"'

'The very same!' Jambo laughed.

Before he could say more, Kurt noticed Louise on her way to find him. 'I'm needed in the kitchen,' he muttered and disappeared.

'This is getting ridiculous,' Kurt thought to himself shortly afterwards, on his own in his bedroom. 'It's Saturday night. There's a great party going on downstairs. Everyone's having a good time and I'm hiding in my room avoiding one girl and wondering what I have to do to get together with another.' He picked up his guitar and began slowly to pick through the notes of one of his own compositions called unsurprisingly 'Can't Get the Girl'.

'Ever been alone in a crowded room
Ever been the stranger on Saturday night
Can't get the girl
Tongue tied not knowin' what to say
Want to get together but can't find the way
Can't get the girl
Can't get the girl . . .'

The melody matched his mood, the words spoke for themselves and, as always, playing his guitar made him feel better. He had just reached the end when Jambo's head appeared round the door. 'I thought you might be hiding yourself in here,' Jambo said. He was dressed in a T-shirt and jeans as usual, his only concession to the party being to swap his khaki T-shirt for one with the 'butter side down' formula on the front.

Jambo guessed rightly what was wrong with Kurt. He lifted one corner of the duvet to peer underneath. 'So, where's Lou . . . Lou . . . Louise?' he asked, never one to be anything other than direct.

Kurt rolled his eyes and shook his head. 'Heavy.'

'I have to say, Benson, I've been surprised, verging on being well impressed,' said Jambo. 'I didn't think she'd last a day.'

'She wasn't supposed to,' Kurt ran his fingers through his hair. 'I have no trouble sorting people but do you remember that time we went shooting rabbits for that farmer . . . ?'

'And you couldn't do it.'

'I just look into those big doleful eyes and she reminds me of a frightened rabbit,' Kurt sighed. 'I can't just dump her. So, I'm open to suggestions.'

'Well I don't fancy here. And whatever you do, she won't be able to face another rejection,' said Jambo.

Jambo was about to get some more to drink when Lucy raced in. Ollie was downstairs with a few of his mates. Kurt jumped up. He was in no mood for messing around. Jambo followed,

'At last – the fight,' he grinned.

In the hall, Tony was standing on one side of the cow with Julie looking anxious behind him. Ollie and three of his mates were on the other side, looking for trouble.

'Just leave it alone, Ollie,' Tony said.

'I just want to know why she binned me for you,' Ollie snarled.

'You know why,' Julie snapped.

It's over, that's all, it happens,' Tony was trying to be reasonable.

'I want to know why,' Ollie shouted at Julie. 'Come on, tell me.'

As Ollie was about to lunge at Julie across the cow, Kurt appeared at the bottom of the stairs. 'Keep out of it, Kurt,' Ollie yelled.

'That's what I told you to do,' Kurt spoke quietly. Lucy and Jambo took up positions on either side of Kurt.

'What are you doing, Ollie?' Lucy also sounded reasonable.

'What's it got to do with you?' Ollie was still shouting.

'If you gatecrash Kurt, you'll gatecrash my parties, too.'

Ollie was puzzled by the logic, 'How can I gatecrash my own home?'

'Because I said you couldn't come,' Kurt was firm.

'In case I upset your mate,' sneered Ollie. His mates stood behind him looking like they wished they were somewhere else.

Kurt grabbed Ollie, 'In case you made a complete dork of yourself, like now.'

Ollie pulled a face. He knew he was on a loser. He said the only thing he could think of, 'I can tell Mum about all this . . .'

Kurt stepped forward, looking furious. Ollie stumbled back.

'Don't be so pathetically childish. Grow up,' Lucy said loudly. Her comment seemed to diffuse the situation. Everyone stood and watched, even the music had died, with Bazz leaning against the living-room door to see what would happen next. Ollie appeared lost. He looked around at Kurt's friends, most of them older than him. He noted the sympathetic glances towards Tony and felt completely out of his depth. Kurt was right. He was acting like a dork.

'I'm going,' he said, but couldn't resist one last jibe at Julie. 'There's too many cows in here.'

At this, Jambo leaped forward and threw his arms around his cow's neck. 'Don't you insult the woman I love,' he yelled.

Everyone laughed. Ollie and his mates left and the party resumed. The music started up again and Bazz announced, 'O.K. pee-op-el. Let's get back on the tracks. It's time for some ree-al music . . .'

'Kurt, you were wonderful,' Louise slipped an arm around Kurt's waist. 'Let's dance. Or do you have to check on something else?'

Just then the doorbell rang. The door was opened and Natasha and Maddie walked in followed by Dawn who looked uncomfortable with Cindy and Max in tow. Louise hurried over to them. Kurt looked surprised to see Cindy and Max. 'What are they doing here?'

Jambo took in Maddie's tightly clad form and grinned at Kurt. 'I'll sort out Maddie for you, if you like.'

'I knew I could count on you,' Kurt said. He glanced across at Natasha. Their eyes locked and he smiled. She smiled back and suddenly the evening seemed worthwhile. Then Louise began to speak to her. Natasha looked uncomfortable. It was decision time. Now or never. He had to sort out Louise. Kurt nodded 'Hello' to Dawn and Maddie but pointed to Louise, then to himself, then upstairs. Louise looked a bit surprised and hesitated. Kurt just grinned and beckoned her to follow him. Louise dashed after him.

Dawn was equally surprised, 'Looks like it might have been a heavenly match after all . . .' She stopped, catching the expression on her friend's face.

Natasha did not look too happy. It had been her joke, she thought it was still a joke but . . . Suppose Dawn was right? She watched Kurt going up the stairs, noticing the gleaming dark-brown hair, the broad shoulders and neat . . . He also looked good in his favourite red shirt. Maybe she had made a big mistake.

Jambo was about to speak to Maddie when she stopped him. 'Drop dead, Bolton.' This did not seem to worry Jambo who turned to Max and Cindy, 'How about the latest computer game?' he asked. Dawn relaxed noticeably and followed on.

Chapter 20

Kurt dashed into his room ahead of Louise and began throwing things around. He flicked drawers open, emptied the dirty laundry from the basket and whisked the bedding off the bed, generally turning the room into a tip.

'Not many people get to see this,' Kurt said as Louise came in.

Louise tried not to wrinkle her nose. 'Do you think we should be in here?' she asked.

'Why not? I live here.'

'What will people think?' Louise giggled. She went to sit down but before she did, Kurt quickly grabbed a dirty sock and threw it on to the chair. She sat down and pulled it out from underneath her dress.

Louise looked at the sock and the rest of the room with distaste. 'You're a bit messy,' she said. Kurt looked hopeful. 'You obviously need someone like me,' she smiled and began to tidy up.

Kurt decided to try a different tack. 'How long is it now? Six days, fourteen hours and twenty-two minutes?'

Louise was impressed that he remembered, but she was looking at his computer.

'What size hard drive do you have – 210, 250?' she asked. Kurt was taken by surprise. 'It's upgraded – two 1.2 gigabytes.'

'SCSI's?'

'Best after 550 . . .'

'Pentium?'

'Nah – went to DX4 after the scare. Haven't upgraded for nine months. You're into computers?'

Louise nodded. 'Got a Toshiba laptop.'

'Cool machines, but I use this mainly for my music now and . . .' Kurt suddenly snapped out of it. He was impressed by Louise's knowledge of computers but that was not the purpose of the exercise. 'So what are we going to do to celebrate out first week?'

'Six days, fourteen hours and,' Louise checked her watch, 'twenty-three minutes.'

Louise picked up a sheet of paper from the desk. Kurt saw what it was and snatched it away. 'It's a note for a song,' he said.

'Is it a love song . . . to me?'

'God no!' Louise looked hurt until Kurt, thinking quickly, added, 'That would take me far longer than six days, fourteen hours and twenty-three minutes.'

'I'd never have guessed you were such a romantic,' Louise flung her arms around his neck and kissed him hard on the lips. When she came up for air, he pulled her close so that at least she wasn't in a position to kiss him again. 'I thought the ouija board was just a stupid idea to humour me. But I think it was the best thing that has ever happened. I think we were made for each other.'

Kurt's face looked pained. But now was the moment of truth. If he was going to act, now was the time. With a deep breath and a sincere expression he looked at Louise and asked seriously, 'Do you really believe that, Louise? That we were made for each other – destined to be together?'

'Oh yes,' Louise sighed.

'That our love will last?'

'Yes!'

'Then why wait any longer?' Kurt threw the bedding back on the bed. He began to unbutton his shirt. 'I've waited six days, fourteen hours and twenty-four minutes,' Kurt checked his watch. 'I don't think I can wait another moment . . .' Louise looked puzzled and stepped back. Kurt pulled her towards him and continued, 'To consummate our love.'

Kurt started to unbuckle his belt. Louise started to panic. 'What!?' she exclaimed.

'You said it yourself – it's destiny,' Kurt reached for the buttons on Louise's dress. She jumped back away from him and edged towards the door.

'Seize the moment, Louise. Grab it while it's there . . . I need you, Louise!'

'I'll seize no such thing. Nor will I grab anything,' Louise had reached the door. 'You need to cool down.' She fled downstairs.

'Ye-es!' Kurt yelled with relief. Buttoning his shirt, he ran downstairs after Louise.

The hall was packed with people and everyone looked very curious. Natasha, Tony and Julie looked shocked. Maddie was intrigued. Everyone followed Kurt as he followed Louise outside.

Kurt was grinning but composed his features when he caught up with her. Louise had needed some fresh air and now chose her words carefully. I'm sorry, Kurt but I can't carry on with this relationship. I'm afraid it's over.'

Kurt could hardly suppress a smile. 'What about the spirits?'

Louise noticed the crowd gathered on the steps. She was not studying drama for nothing. This was her big performance. Drawing herself up to her full height she explained. 'That was only an indication of who my next boyfriend would be, not how long that relationship would be and certainly not what type of relationship it should be.'

Kurt was also playing to the crowd. 'You mean it's . . . over?' he said dramatically.

'Yes. And although it was only six days, fourteen hours and twenty-six minutes,' Louise now looked at her watch, 'I hope you felt it was worthwhile.'

'Yeah – a blast.'

Louise kissed his cheek and smiled reassuringly. 'And don't worry. Time is a great healer. There's always plenty more fish in the sea.' She walked back into the house and the crowd started to melt away, now the drama was over.

'Nice one, Benson,' Maddie smiled. 'Need a bosom to cry on?'

Kurt said he would let her know. He waited for her to go back inside before he turned to Natasha, who was waiting for him on the steps. Kurt raised his eyebrows at her. She smiled. He smiled.

'That was neat,' Natasha said.

'Louise had to make the decision to junk me,' Kurt shrugged. Natasha nodded. She understood the logic.

'I wondered what was going on at first,' she began. 'I'm sorry I landed you with her. But it was what she needed and – it was a very nice thing for you to have done. I'm almost impressed,' Natasha chewed her lip, feeling suddenly shy. Neither of them was sure what to say next.

'It's only left me in emotional trauma,' Kurt joked and held out his arms. 'As mad Maddie said, I'm in need of a bit of comfort and support.'

'What would people think if I moved in so soon on my girlfriend's ex?' Natasha teased.

Kurt laughed. 'So how long do I have to wait?'

'Longer than your involvement with Louise,' Natasha grinned.

Kurt paused two seconds. 'O.K. That was it.'

Natasha laughed. 'Longer than she thinks you were involved.'

'How about six days, fourteen hours and twenty-seven minutes?' Kurt gazed into her eyes.

'Maybe . . .' Natasha, smiling, gazed back.